LOVE IS THE JEWEL

What is Julie Quinn running away from? What memory has haunted her so that she will not talk about the accident that lamed her and took her as an outpatient at Elronstock Hospital? Adam Hollidge, the surgeon at the hospital manages to win her confidence, but, before Julie can tell him everything, Boyd Marwick re-enters her life and shatters her new-found hopes of peace. Who is he, and how is he connected with Julie?

LOVE IS THE JEWEL

Love Is The Jewel

by

Jane Lester

Dales Large Print Books
Long Preston, North Yorkshire,
BD23 4ND, England.

British Library Cataloguing in Publication Data.

Lester, Jane
   Love is the jewel.

   A catalogue record of this book is
   available from the British Library

   ISBN   978-1-84262-869-0 pbk

First published in Great Britain in 1966 by Robert Hale Ltd.

Copyright © Jane Lester 1966

Cover illustration © Ruby Del Angel by arrangement with
Arcangel Images

The moral right of the author has been asserted

Published in Large Print 2011 by arrangement with
S. Walker Literary Agency

Dales Large Print is an imprint of Library Magna Books Ltd.

Printed and bound in Great Britain by
T.J. (International) Ltd., Cornwall, PL28 8RW

CHAPTER ONE

Julie Quinn left the Out-Patients' Department of the Eltonstock General Hospital that day, wondering if she would bother to come again. It was only because that new surgeon had insisted that, given time, she would be back to normal, that she had kept attending the big gleaming new hospital, with its white walls reflecting the glare of the sunshine, and every one of its big windows shining like the jewels under the glass cases in the shop where she worked.

She yearned to be the same again. To run for that bus which she must now lose because she just wasn't quick enough. To play tennis again, and to swim. On days such as this, with the sky that hurting blue, she longed to be able to put back the clock to the time before the accident had happened.

She shied away from the thought of it, and concentrated instead on the new surgeon. What was he like? She couldn't find words to describe him. He was one of those pleasant ordinary people one would never look twice at, never remember on meeting the second time. Pale straw coloured hair, not particularly straight, not wavy, but the sort that kept tidy. Steady eyes (she remembered their steadiness but she couldn't remember their colour) and a face that had no particular feature; not even a moustache to make him different from the next man. An ordinary face. In a world of long white coats, he mingled and was lost in the crowd. Yet there had been *something* about him. What was it?

She concentrated on trying to remember the one thing that made him so different from everyone else in the Out-Patients' department, while she sat on the seat in the bus yard, waiting for the next bus back to Fleckbury. Oh, yes, it was his voice.

That kindly, strong voice, that said things and made you believe them, such as that one must forget the unpleasant details of the accident, but yet not run away from the sight or sound of a motor-bike. That way led to disaster. You couldn't hide from the things that hurt you, he had told her. You had to have patience; the good things came slowly. You had to have faith in the people who were trying to help you.

Well, she had faith in him, and she supposed she would keep on coming over to Eltonstock every week in spite of the difficulty of the journey; in spite of having to get time off from a new job, and convincing her new employers that it was worthwhile. In spite of the myriad terrors she suffered every time she saw an ambulance or heard the sudden sharp shrill scream of brakes, she would come.

She would come only because of the new surgeon, the man who was just a voice in her mind because she couldn't remember his face – the man whose name she had never heard.

Her bus came in at last. She was so late, she would have to work through part of her lunch hour to make up for this lost time.

She climbed painfully to the top deck, because she didn't like travelling inside, and she sat watching the crowds on the pavement, the massed traffic in the road around the bus, cranes on a building site; the banners of a demonstration marching in the gutter, workmen with pneumatic drills making a hole in the road, crowds of people forcing their way through the packed traffic – as if it were all part of a hideous dream. With every sharp sudden noise, and every crowd of people, she was always afraid it was another street accident, yet she had to come up on to the top deck and look at it all. She dare not go inside and close her eyes to it.

She hated Eltonstock. Hated the lurid posters on the high hoardings, the flat uninteresting shop-fronts, the drab grey walls everywhere, and the way the few churches were hemmed in by commercial buildings.

If she had anything to be thankful for, in

this uprooting of herself from her home town, so many miles away, it was for having discovered Fleckbury, where she now lived and worked.

She thought about her job, and of how the hours of standing would affect her, but as she had explained to the hospital people, it was what she had been trained for. What she hadn't said was that the thought of being in a sit-down job, in a small office or factory, was unbearable. Since the accident, she had felt that trapped sensation too often. To be behind a counter of a shop offered freedom of movement, and although she couldn't go out into the street very often, she was able to if a customer wanted to point out something in the window. It was the thought of that flash of freedom, the fresh air flowing on her face, that kept her going.

She was aware of her own reflection in the bus window. An interesting rather than a pretty face, with soft light-brown hair (cut now in a thick fringe to hide a new scar) with a longish boy's cut at the back. It suited her, went with the saucy little nose. It was, normally, a face quick to smile.

The customers liked that little face. It had a can-I-help-you look which was coupled with a warmth and friendliness that was rather endearing. She had worked in a jewellery department of a big store before she had come to Fleckbury, so the work wasn't entirely new. She had gravitated from there to the manager's office because they had discovered she could type quickly and accurately, but that was a thing she hadn't mentioned in this new job.

She had just come to the part where she was telling herself firmly that she liked her new job and liked Fleckbury and didn't regret anything, when the bus swung round into the square and it was time to get off. An ordeal, always, getting down those stairs, trying not to appear to be clinging to the rails because she was afraid of being jerked downwards. Trying desperately to appear just the same as the other passengers but taking her time...

Somehow, that morning, the shop seemed a refuge. There was no sound of footsteps in the lush carpet that covered the floor. The men (Julie was the only girl on the staff) still wore, from time immemorial, pin-striped trousers, black jackets, stiff collars. Mr Howe, the old gentleman, liked it, although he was seldom there these days. And they all spoke in muted voices.

'Why are you late, Miss Quinn?' old Mr Wexibole asked her under his breath. There were customers in the shop.

In the same tone she reminded him of her hospital trip.

'Ah, yes, I recall,' he whispered. 'Go and get ready quickly. We require your assistance.'

She went quietly to remove her outer things. Mr Wexibole was fussy but essentially a kind old man.

In such a little while she was ready, behind her counter, safe and secure from the noisy world of Eltonstock for another week – that noisy world that conjured up memories of past days she wanted to forget.

And then *he* came out from behind a screen and stood at a point where he could see her: the new young man who had been about the shop for the past two weeks.

Julie wished he wouldn't keep watching her. He was tall, lean, distinguished; his long, thin face was tanned, and the dark colour of his skin emphasised the blue of his eyes. They didn't just look – they bored through her. And at the very least thing, those expressive eyebrows of his would jerk up, speaking volumes. No doubt he had a good reason for being there, but she wished he hadn't. It was all very fine to be warned that there would be a store detective about and as this was a jeweller's, it was more than likely that he would be keeping his eye on the newest employee but she was nervous enough already.

She tried to concentrate on the things she had been told. Everything in the more popular ranges was clearly marked but if a customer wanted a really good article, Julie was to refer him to someone else; someone like old Mr Gooch, who had been in the firm for almost sixty years, or like Mr Wexibole, whose beetling white brows and beard always intimidated Julie in spite of his kind manner to her.

Emeralds and rubies glistened under plate glass, and there was a diamond tiara that kept catching the sunshine and sending out blue shafts of fire. But for Julie there were only the reasonably priced canteens of cutlery, the modest gold and silver wrist watches, the nice little pearl necklaces, the pendants and crucifixes.

A customer came in at that moment. A young woman, bothered about the choice of a gift for her aunt, she said. Together she and Julie pored over a tray of marquisite dress clips. Still undecided, the young woman finally said she would think it over and come back.

Conscious of the young man standing staring across at her all the time, Julie picked up the tray to put it back under the glass counter. She had almost got it there when her fingers fumbled, and it fell, tipping its contents all over the floor.

Julie felt that everyone in the shop was looking at her, as, scarlet of face, she bent to pick them up. But it was only old Mr Gooch who came over to her.

'Is anything wrong, Miss Quinn?' he asked her softly, as he bent over the counter to look at what she was doing. 'Bless me, how did that happen?'

'I'm so sorry, Mr Gooch, but I get so nervous – that young man keeps looking at me as if he is afraid I shall make off with something when no one is looking,' Julie said, rising from the floor with a flushed countenance.

Mr Gooch permitted himself a slight smile as he helped her to replace the now re-filled tray in its proper place. 'Don't concern yourself over him, my dear young lady. That is our Mr Stannard. Mr Neville Stannard,' he repeated, as if it were something special.

Julie tried to look suitably impressed. 'Well, I suppose he has to look after the goods in the store, but I wish you'd tell him I'm quite honest, and I have worked in a jeweller's before.'

'We know that,' Mr Gooch said, in a rebuking kind of voice. 'We know that your references are excellent, or else you wouldn't have been employed here in the first place. And do try to remember that this is not a jewellery *store*. It is Howe's the Jeweller.'

Howe's the Jeweller. In Fleckbury that was something, Julie knew. And she had to go on living in Fleckbury, at least for the time being. It was a haven of refuge – there would be peace of mind here, because it was very unlikely that Boyd Markwick would think of looking for her in a small town like this.

Fleckbury lay in a fold of the hills, a prim little Edwardian town that was, if not exactly behind the times, then certainly not bang up to the minute. A town that went its peaceful way without bothering to wonder if the world outside had heard of it before. A town uncluttered by posters, a town that was patronised by elderly people who wanted a quiet stay in a good family hotel where the food was reliable, and – for the menfolk at least – some good fishing. The River Fleck ran down from St Agnes, the big hill shaped like a sugar loaf, and meandered through the town under its five bridges. Artists came to paint it, and not once had Julie heard, in the night, the roar of a motor-bike. For that, at least, she was grateful. She never wanted to hear a motor-bike again and she never wanted to see Boyd or his friends any more.

She still walked with a very slight limp since the accident. On good days it was hardly noticeable. On a day such as today, when she was already nervous, it was painfully clear that she didn't walk quite like other people.

She tried to hurry, as she left the shop for her lunch, because above all, she didn't want that tiresome young man to come striding after her, but he caught her up before she reached the Copper Kettle after all.

The lights changed just as she reached the

small side road where the half-timbered building housing the best home-cooked food in the town, straddled on its narrow pavement.

She still wasn't used to curbing her impatience, waiting for the road to completely clear because she could no longer dart across. She began to make a dash for it, as the traffic started to move, and her bad leg gave way. She would have pitched forward in the path of the oncoming taxis and cars, if a strong arm hadn't gone round her, literally lifting her back to safety.

'Steady on. That was a silly thing to do,' a familiar voice said, and Julie looked furiously up into the face of Neville Stannard, whose eyebrows were raised in eloquent shock that a young woman with such an intelligent face could be so silly.

'I'm sorry,' she muttered.

'Good gracious, don't apologise. Just thank your lucky stars that I happened to be close enough to help you. Now, you could do with a nip of something to stop you shaking.'

He glanced round the busy lunch-time streets, spotted an opening in the traffic large enough to give her time to cross comfortably and led her down an alley to the car park.

'But I just wanted to go over the road to the Copper Kettle,' Julie protested. 'I wanted a quick lunch because I'm working extra time– I was late this morning, you see.'

'Oh, rubbish, come and have lunch with me, then I can make sure you have something a little stronger than milky coffee with it.'

Her leg began to throb, so she let him have his own way. She was glad enough to get into the car he unlocked – a small but practical pale blue model – and sit back with her eyes closed.

'Where are we going?' she asked him.

'Only to the other side of the town. I know just the place for a nice quiet meal.'

'Shouldn't you be on duty? Who's going to watch people while you're taking me to lunch?' she asked him.

He looked blank, so she amplified: 'Well, that's what a store detective is for, isn't it – to watch people?'

'Oh, I see,' he said, and then something seemed to amuse him very much. 'You were quick,' he told her. 'I shouldn't let it get around, though. You were pretty nippy at spotting what I was up to, but I wouldn't want everyone to know.'

No, she thought, Howe's the Jeweller was a firm who would consider themselves above adopting the methods of the department stores in combating theft. They might even consider themselves above the attention of shoplifters even, but it looked as if events must have proved otherwise in the past. The subject was not one that she liked. Her heart beat an uneasy tattoo.

Stop it, she told herself fiercely. That's all over. All in the past. And you had nothing to do with it, you fool.

She glanced at Neville Stannard. He was watching the traffic all around him, assessing it, seizing an opportunity to slip into a gap at the kerb, to slide into the forecourt of Fleckbury's largest hotel, the Carlton. She waited quietly while he locked the car, uncomfortably aware that she was still white and inclined to be shaky, but it wasn't entirely through her bad judgment when he had rescued her from the traffic. It was mainly through her frightening thoughts.

'You still look pale,' he said, looking critically at her. 'Let's see about that drink.'

She felt better after it. They followed the head waiter to a pleasant table in a corner, and she relaxed under the influence of good food and Neville's unexpectedly easy manner. He was altogether different now, and even his eyebrows weren't so intimidating.

'Do you like working in Fleckbury?' he asked her.

'Yes, it's a nice quiet place,' she admitted.

'But you miss London,' he guessed. 'Don't look so surprised. I know the details on the card in the cabinet. Well, as a store detective, I would have to know all about the employees, wouldn't I?'

'What else do you know about me?' she asked, trying to remember how much she had been forced to tell about herself on joining the firm.

'Nothing very terrible,' he assured her. 'I know that you are only twenty-two, which seems very young when viewed from my years.' That made a smile break over her face, so he said quickly, 'I'm six years older than you, young lady,' and he laughed, he was so glad that that frozen look was leaving her now. 'And I know also that your full name is Julie Augusta Rianon Quinn, you were born in Wales, and lived most of your life in London, that you are an orphan, an only child, and in short a rather lonely little person.'

'Not really lonely,' she denied quickly. 'I just like being on my own.'

'Rather an odd desire for someone quite so pretty and young,' he observed. 'The card wasn't complete, anyway. There was nothing on it about that limp or what you'd been doing for the last four months, before you joined us.'

'Oh, so that's why you came after me! I thought you were being kind but it wasn't that at all. My card didn't give a full history, so you thought you'd be clever and get the rest of the details this way. Rather an expensive way of going about it, isn't it?' and

19

she glanced significantly around her.

'Don't be silly, Julie. Besides, it isn't true. The references have been passed, anyway. We have no right to ask you for any more details.'

She disliked his use of the word 'we' as if he were actually in the confidence of Mr Howe, the head of the firm, whom Julie hadn't even seen. Who did Neville Stannard think he was? A store detective – an employee, just like herself!

'Now you're looking all cross again,' he complained. 'If I've put it clumsily, do forgive me, but honestly, I only wanted to be friends. I've been watching you since you joined us–'

'Don't I know it,' she couldn't resist saying.

'And I saw an intelligent young woman who is already winning the confidence of the customers. A young woman who will probably do very well at her new job, but I am not sure if standing all day on a leg that lets you down in the street, is a wise thing to do. Was it an accident, by the way?'

The abruptness of the question took her by surprise.

'Yes, it was,' she admitted.

'Then you'd better learn to be more patient in crossing the road if you don't want it to happen again, hadn't you?' he said gently.

He was really very nice, she thought. When he forgot to be Mr Eagle-Eye or Mr

Friend-of-the-Boss, she reminded herself indignantly.

'It might be possible for you to sit down between customers. You have only to mention your accident, you know. Mr Gooch is a very kind old man, and he seems to like you. He wouldn't mind, if you explained the situation to him.'

She shrugged. 'I mustn't allow myself to become soft. I've undertaken to serve behind a counter,' and she resolutely wouldn't permit herself to notice him wincing at this description of her work at Howe's. 'So I must get used to it.'

'Didn't you do that sort of work at your last job, then?'

Again she shrugged. 'I did secretarial work as well.'

'Did you? That wasn't on your card either. Why wasn't it?'

'What good would it have done? You know the firm just wanted an extra person behind the counter.'

'How do you know there may not be another opening later?' he asked in exasperation. 'What else can you do besides secretarial work?'

'You really want to know?' A puckish smile broke over her face. 'I have a sizeable knowledge of gems and their history, and I know a lot about the inner secrets of police and private detectives.'

21

She was rewarded by his stare of pure astonishment. 'Really? You mean you've had special training to that end?'

'No. I just read it up. I happened to lodge over a second-hand bookshop and my landlady's brother used to let me have the run of the shop and he helped me to search out special books. He was almost like family to me. He was a dear,' she finished in a low voice.

Neville Stannard was at once interested, so she forestalled any further questions in that direction by saying shortly, 'He died. In a road accident. The business was sold. I had to move on.'

She might have added that Reuben Floy had been killed in the same accident that had left her with a limp, but she didn't. That would have made an opening for more questions, painful questions. She had had enough. She got up.

'Thank you for the lunch, Mr Stannard. It was very kind of you, but I had really better be getting back to the shop.'

He nodded and said, thinking, 'All right. Just wait while I settle the bill. Oh, and while I think of it – don't go tonight till I bring my car round from the car park. I'll drive you home. You must have a bit of sense after that shock you sustained at the traffic lights today.'

'Oh, but I'll be all right by then. You don't

have to feel responsible for me,' she protested.

'Don't argue,' he laughed, beckoning the waiter. 'Go and powder your nose or something.'

He didn't want her to see him paying for the lunch, she decided, so she walked away to the Ladies Room. There were big mirrors on the wall. In one of them she saw Neville Stannard settling the bill, not by cash but by signing the account. And the waiter hovered as if he were someone important, not just the store detective.

It worried her. Living beyond his means, pretending to be someone grand. She had seen that happen before, and that way led to trouble. She would have to keep clear of him.

A way presented itself of avoiding him, when it neared closing time. He was called to the telephone in the office. She could hear his voice, and the grand manner was there again. She glanced at Mr Gooch and Mr Wexibole, but they didn't seem to be listening. The other men on the staff were busy putting trays of gems away, the two older men superintending. Julie gave up the problem, but taking advantage of Neville Stannard being still on the telephone, she put on her coat, quietly said good night to the others, and went home.

'Home' was No 16 Canary Lane. A quiet

little cul-de-sac behind the church. The garden was a mass of flowers. Her landlady's husband kept it going. He had been injured in a railway accident, and had bought the little house with his compensation. He lived for his flowers. He was in the front garden fussing with the miniature pool he had made. He looked up with a smile.

'Hello, Mr Leigh, still at it,' Julie said, and paused to inspect his work.

'Aye,' he said. He looked helplessly pleased. He hadn't a great fund of words, and just waved a hand vaguely around to embrace the extra stones he had put into place that day, the new pieces of rock plant he had set between them, and the netting anchored across the top to protect the fish from marauding local cats until the pond weed could grow enough to give them shelter. All this he wanted to convey to Julie, but he could only stand and smile at his handiwork.

'I think it's going to be most attractive,' Julie said firmly. 'It really has a professional touch about it.'

He looked so overwhelmed at her praise that even his smile vanished, only to break out again wider than ever.

His wife made up for his inarticulate state. 'Gideon, where are you?' she called. 'If there's one thing I can't abide it's when I cook you a nice tea and you don't come and here I am standing by the stove looking a perfect fool, wondering how to keep the food hot and not knowing if you've even heard me. What are you doing, I'd like to know? If you're in that garden again I shall have something to say about it. You make a body near almost to praying for hail and snow, that you do, so's you'd be forced to stay in the house for once, and then I suppose you'd be off and away up to the attic to look over those old gardening books you still keep up there. Don't tell me you threw them out – I know you didn't, even though I've asked you again and again but do you ever do anything I want?'

Gideon caught Julie's eye as he called out in reply to his wife. He shook his head, half apologetically, and offered: 'Vera, she do run on. Can't help it.'

Julie nodded in an attempt to convey that she understood. 'We'd better go in, hadn't we?' she said.

They went, quietly. Fellow-conspirators. He looked down at her leg and asked quietly, 'Bad day?'

She nodded. She didn't mind Gideon asking. He was a fellow sufferer. He still went to the General Hospital in Eltonstock for a regular check-up. 'Almost got run over again,' she told him. 'Don't mention it to Mrs Leigh, will you?'

'No, she'll worry,' Gideon agreed. It was a

pleasant fiction between them and it merely meant that Mrs Leigh would have a great deal to say about people who had already had an accident and didn't take enough sensible care of themselves afterwards.

Still, Vera Leigh was a good cook. Even the simple meal of egg and bacon and sausage flan sent out dream-like smells to the hungry. Gideon and Julie scrubbed up in record time and sat down meekly at the kitchen table.

'So you've come at last,' Vera observed. To Julie, she added, 'That man! Don't get married, dear. Take my word for it, it's not worth it. Men, they're more trouble than they're worth. I always tell my young lady lodgers never to contemplate it. Stay single, I say, and you won't get grey hairs so quick. Men!'

She dished up generous helpings of vegetables grown in Gideon's vegetable patch, and poured handsome portions of good thick gravy made from stock. It didn't matter what the meal was, there was always a good gravy to go with it, and while she served up, she talked non-stop.

'Speaking of men, what happened at the hospital today, dear? Did they say anything could be done? Mind you, I've no great faith in these fellows – give 'em a chance to cut you about, and they've got you on the operating table before you can say Jack Robinson, but it's as I always say to Gideon here –

once you've been bashed about, it's up to you to see they do what they can to put you right again. When are they going to do something?'

'They didn't say definitely,' Julie admitted. 'I don't always see the same person. There's a young man with glasses–'

'That sounds like Peter Lawrence, wouldn't you say, Gideon?' Vera put in knowledgeably. She knew all of the surgeons at the hospital because of Gideon's regular attendance over the years.

Gideon nodded, and Vera went on, 'What did you say was the name of that new man who was so good. Horrocks, wasn't it? Something like that, Gideon? Bless the man, he's off in a dream about his garden again. *Gideon!*'

'Hollidge,' Gideon said. 'Adam Hollidge. You want to try and see him,' he told Julie.

'What's the good of telling her she ought to try and see him?' Mrs Leigh scolded. 'You know very well everyone has to see who they're sent to, and if this new man isn't there, why then, they all get sent to someone else. Like a lot of sheep,' she finished angrily.

'Peter Lawrence is a good man, I've heard,' Julie said pacifically. 'But he doesn't think much can be done, but the other man – this Mr Hollidge – is very hopeful. I didn't even know his name, but I expect that's who it is. Sort of light hair and nothing special about him, but his voice is the sort that just makes you want to go on listening to him.'

'That'll be him all right,' Vera Leigh said positively, beginning to gather the dinner plates almost before her husband and Julie had finished. 'That's a very good description. Charm a bird off a tree with that voice, he would. Mind you, he's a somebody. They do say he could be in London – in Harley Street – if he had a mind to, only he's taken up with Eltonstock Hospital. Can't think why. If ever there was a dreary town, that's Eltonstock. And that hospital gives me the creeps, it's so big and cold and new, all shiny metal and paint and tiles.'

She cut up wedges of Bakewell Tart and passed the plates round. 'You can always see the names, you know, if you look up on the board above the seats. Custard, dear?'

'Yes, please, and I did look at the board, but the name hadn't been put in, the last time. He was the only one on duty and we were all sent over to his batch of seats.'

'That's them all over. You never know where you are with them. And you'll have to keep on at them or they'll be saying the same as they did to Gideon here, that they'd send for him when the time was ripe, and they never did another thing. Look at the time he wastes, going over to that hospital for his check-ups. No, well, I know he doesn't have to go every week, the same as you do, but he has to go enough, to my way of thinking. And you watch out, dear, or they'll stop it being once a week, and it'll get to once a month and then once in six months, and then you'll hear no more about it, and you don't want to go limping through life, a pretty girl like you, do you? You ought to be going cycling with the gang, or dancing and such. What *is* it, Gideon?' she broke off to say impatiently.

Gideon hadn't any words to frame his embarrassment. He could only look in mute appeal at his wife and then at Julie's downcast face as she stared at her plate and tried to keep the tears from scorching her eyes. Limping through life. Yes, that just about described her, she thought in dismay, as she remembered her performance that morning, when the good-looking Neville Stannard had rescued her. Limping through life.

CHAPTER TWO

Neville Stannard was cross with Julie the next day.

'Why didn't you wait for me last night?' he demanded.

'You were busy. It didn't really matter, did it? I mean, it was a kind thought, if you

29

hadn't been otherwise engaged.'

He looked exasperated and then he burst out laughing.

'You are a queer girl. Kind thought indeed. I wanted to drive you home. Does that mean anything to you? My dear girl, a chap doesn't ask to drive a girl home because he is feeling kind, you may take it from me.'

'Then why did you want to drive me home?' she persisted.

'Have you never been walked home or driven home before? Don't tell me you've never had anyone interested in you, because I refuse to believe that.'

'Of course I have before I hurt my leg. I used to go dancing and swimming and playing tennis. But I can't do any of those things now, so of what use to offer to drive me home?'

'Bless the girl,' he complained. 'There are many young women who are too lazy or incompetent to do any of those things, and they still get by,' he said mildly, half-smiling at her.

'I don't doubt it, but then, do you see, they could do those things if they put their mind to it.'

'So many objections to a simple request from me to take you home in my car. What's the matter, don't you like me? Is that what you're trying to say?' he asked bluntly.

'Of course not. I like you, Mr Stannard, so

far as that goes. But I hardly know you, do I?'

'And you wouldn't object to getting to know me better? Is that the case?'

'I suppose so,' she said helplessly. 'But I really ought to be on my counter,' she reminded him.

'All right, but tonight, then? A nice innocuous drive somewhere and a bite to eat? Or perhaps you'd like to see a film?'

'All right,' she agreed, without enthusiasm.

He let her go, and old Mr Gooch went up to him to speak to him. Julie got out a tray of cuff-links to show to a customer and forgot about Neville Stannard.

At lunch time, however, she remembered it, and her uneasiness was renewed. It wasn't entirely true to say that she liked him. Her liking was tempered with doubt, because so many things about him were hard to explain away. Considering he was only one of the staff, he sometimes acted as if he were someone quite important. He was good-looking, young, and with a good appearance, but that didn't justify (in Julie's opinion) his taking a girl out of the shop to the sort of place to eat which might be used by the boss himself. And Neville Stannard was much too free with his money. Free in the way he splashed it around, as if he had more than he need to worry about, and that, of course, just didn't make sense.

31

Julie had had enough of young men who lived beyond their means; who existed in a dream world. The result was the same; they came to a sticky end and dragged down any unfortunate girl who happened to be friendly with them.

She thought of Boyd Markwick and his friends, and shuddered. No, she had got away from all that. She just wanted to live a simple life, with no complications in the form of a good-looking store detective who appeared to have too much money.

On her way back to the shop, Neville Stannard appeared from nowhere and announced that he would walk back with her.

She didn't realise how reluctant she looked at this suggestion.

'What's the matter, Julie? You *don't* like me, do you?' he insisted. 'I wish you'd come right out with it and be frank and honest with me.'

'Well, I don't want to be taken to expensive places like the last time, if I go out with you at all,' she said at last.

'Oh, is that all? What's the objection to the poor old Carlton? I thought you'd like it.'

'I did. I mean, it worried me because you shouldn't be throwing your money about like that. I'm putting this awfully badly, but you're just an employee like myself, and I would have been quite happy with a snack in a milk bar.'

'But if I'd been well-off, you'd have expected to be taken to a place like that?' he wanted to know.

'Yes, I suppose so.'

'Would it make you feel any better if I told you that I'm not hard up – that I don't have to rely on what I earn at Howe's? And that I truly loved taking you to nice places to eat?'

'Would it be the truth?'

'Funny little Julie, of course it would.'

'Then in that case I suppose it's all right,' she allowed.

'Good. Then that's settled. And you'll let me take you out tonight? And no questions about whether I can afford it?'

'All right,' she smiled.

Having been genuinely convinced at last, Julie dismissed her doubts and found it rather pleasant to feel that she could look forward to be taken out again.

It seemed a long, long time since she had last been dated. She wondered what she would wear, and then she recalled that he wasn't giving her time to go home and change. It was too late to ask him now, but there must be an opportunity to speak to him about it later.

She didn't see him in the lunch hour. He seemed to have vanished. Nowadays he didn't watch her so much, but moved about the shop and sometimes stayed out of sight altogether. It was all very puzzling.

When she came back from lunch, he still wasn't in sight, and because she was really anxious about changing into something suitable for the kind of place he would take her to, after this morning's discussion, she ventured to ask Mr Gooch where he could be found.

Mr Gooch looked faintly shocked.

'What do you want to speak to our Mr Stannard for, young lady?' he asked, in his fussy, old-fashioned way.

'It was a personal matter, but it can't really wait,' Julie stammered. Something about Mr Gooch's manner bothered her, as if Neville Stannard was too important for her to approach first hand. But what was so special about a detective employed in the store?

'Never mind, perhaps I'll see him about the shop later,' she said, and smiled her thanks.

Mr Gooch wasn't satisfied. 'It is hardly your place to try to engage Mr Stannard in conversation. Tell me what it is you want. After all, young lady, that's what I'm here for, to answer queries from everyone.'

So what was it, she thought. The poor old thing thought he was being by-passed. 'Well, I don't suppose it matters if you know,' Julie said, shrugging and smiling, 'though I know you can't help, because it *is* personal. You see, we're friends outside the firm, and tonight—'

She got no further. She broke off in sheer surprise, because Mr Gooch's eyebrows shot up and his eyes popped. He pursed his lips as if he were blowing something tiresome away, and said quickly, 'Our Mr Stannard? Friends outside? Oh, no, no, my dear young lady, that won't do at all. Mr Howe would never approve. Never.'

Julie thought he meant that Mr Howe (who was something of a legendary figure to the staff) disapproved of employees mixing and spending off-time together. She frowned, but realised it was no use going any further with the subject, for poor old Mr Gooch was so dyed-in-the-wool, he just wouldn't understand.

'Never mind, I'll speak to him later,' she said, and went back to her counter.

It was a quiet afternoon so Mr Wexibole kindly let her help him dust the cases of the important pieces, with one of the other assistants 'standing by' as the old man called it.

This was something of a ceremony. The big case was circular in shape with a metal mesh guard under the glass, so that the contents could be seen every day but their safety was assured. Each night a contingent of the older staff bore the contents of this case to the big safe in the inner office.

'This is the Mendellini Collar,' Mr Wexibole told Julie importantly. 'It was made up to special order for a customer who never claimed it, because the poor lady was killed in a plane accident.'

'What happens to pieces that aren't bought after they've been specially ordered? Does it happen often?' Julie asked.

'Normally,' Mr Wexibole explained, looking nettled, 'they are broken down and re-made up. But this piece was of such fine workmanship that it is kept here as an advertisement of what can be done here – not, of course, that Howe's *needs* advertisement, but it was such loving workmanship, it would be a thousand pities to break it down again. See the grading of the gems and the clever massing of colours to form a flower pattern.'

Julie privately thought it was hideous. It wasn't her taste at all, but she supposed that if you were rich and elderly like most of the important customers of the firm, it was the sort of thing you would want to wear. 'It looks like something out of a history book,' she said, feeling that some comment was required of her.

Mr Wexibole looked delighted. 'Yes, my dear young lady, that is just where the inspiration was first found. From a picture of a Dutch princess of the Middle Ages – improved on, of course, by the customer, advised by the firm, of course.'

The other young man – one of the newer members of the staff, was winking behind Mr Wexibole's back, and later, when he had a chance to get Julie to herself, he said privately, 'That glass case is called the Morgue (only don't let the old boy hear you say so) because all those pieces were made specially and not taken up. The firm don't like it, but they daren't refuse important customers.'

'Are you sure?' Julie asked.

He nodded. 'You must be a greenhorn to believe all old Wexibole tells you. That Collar was designed for an American – made his pile in soft drinks and ice cream – wanted it for his missus.'

Julie looked at him in distaste. He had tried more than once to impress her with how much he knew about the trade, and what a smart one he was.

'You're joking, Mr Carr. The Mendellini Collar?'

'That's right. Don't be misled by its posh name. The ice-cream johnny was named Mendellini – started out with an ice-cream parlour in the Bronx and made his pile. Wouldn't think it to hear old Wexibole, would you? Still, I suppose the old boy can be forgiven his swanking about it, because the rumour's going round that he's got a bite.'

'A bite?' she repeated blankly.

'A nibble. From a duchess. Well, if you want it in Wexibole jargon, Her Grace has expressed the first faint glimmerings of interest in such a manner that one may be forgiven the anticipation of a future arrangement.'

His mimicry of Mr Wexibole was excellent. Julie turned away to hide a smile.

'In other words, he's going to get rid of the Mendellini Collar on the old girl for as many thousands as he can screw out of her. Well, why not? Mr Howe doesn't know what's going on, and he wouldn't care if he did.'

'Where *is* Mr Howe, then?' Julie asked. Sometimes she had the feeling that there wasn't a Mr Howe. That his name was just used to impress people, especially young members of the staff.

'Don't you know?' Charlie Carr laughed. 'Oh, look out – here comes old Wexibole.'

He melted away behind a show-case and the next Julie saw of him, he was doing his polished best to persuade a reluctant elderly lady to buy a grandmother clock.

At tea-time, Julie saw Neville Stannard come in. Today he was so different, and never glanced her way once. Yet he must have been aware of her standing behind her counter.

Before she could even try to catch his eye, Mr Gooch went forward and engaged him in conversation. For a moment Julie wondered if he might be remonstrating with Neville Stannard about his friendship with Julie, but Mr Gooch appeared rather deferential in his manner. Julie remembered that Mr Gooch usually did when he spoke to that young man.

The first time she was free, she was determined to go and speak to him. He was standing by the circular showcase, pointing to the collar and questioning Mr Wexibole. Mr Wexibole went away and Neville was alone.

He looked up as Julie limped down the expanse of the carpeted showroom towards him. She felt that everyone must be looking at her and she wished he would help her out by coming towards her.

He smiled faintly at her, then his glance shifted to the door, with a look of recognition for the person just coming in from the street.

'Just a minute,' he said to Julie and hurried past her, a huge smile dawning on his face.

Julie looked round to see a young woman sail in. A uniformed chauffeur, who had been holding the door open for her, backed out, and Mr Gooch ineffectually tried to beat Neville in getting first to the girl to escort her. When he realised he wasn't going to be quick enough, Mr Gooch halted, and gave a stiff little bow instead – the sort they gave to very important customers.

The young woman was tall and good-looking in a statuesque way. Her blonde hair was almost out of sight beneath an extremely *chic* hat, and her *couturière* dress of very pale green was matched by shoes exactly the same shade and neither came from the Fleckbury shops. She wore a mink stole, and wafted expensive perfume as she walked.

'Darling,' she said to Neville, in a syrupy voice that managed to make itself heard everywhere, 'Daddy wants me to choose something for my birthday. It's an awful bore, but I have to play up to the poor old thing.'

Julie faded to behind her counter again, her cheeks hot. He might have saved her from being in that ignominious position. What was he doing, having a wealthy customer calling him fancy names in a loud voice, and how was it Mr Gooch allowed it? Or was it a friend of Neville's just buying from the shop? Neville, she recalled, had insisted that he wasn't entirely dependent on what he earned in the shop, but did his private income put him on 'darling' terms with people like that girl? And if so, what did he want to go out of his way to be friends with the newest employee for, Julie asked herself furiously.

Ignoring Charlie Carr's wicked grin and gleam of interest, as he stood watching the proceedings, Julie tidied her shelves (though they didn't really need it) and took herself to task over Neville. No wonder Mr Gooch had been shocked. To him, Julie reflected, such a friendship as hers and Neville's would be quite unsuitable. Well, was it quite suitable from her own point of view? All right, no one cared about such things nowadays, and Howe's the Jeweller's was a hopelessly outdated firm and the old employees really weren't in this world.

Just the same, if Julie were out with Neville and that girl saw him and joined them, what would her manner be to Julie? Julie couldn't imagine her screaming 'darling' and being as pleased to see her as she had evidently been just now to see Neville.

The girl was in the inner sanctum. She would be sitting in the big padded chair with the black velvet unrolled on the table top. V.I.P. treatment for special customers. Would she be looking at the Mendellini Collar? That case hadn't been unlocked, and Julie was pretty sure that that girl's taste would run to delicate fine workmanship, not flamboyant stuff like the Collar. Besides, the Collar had been designed to cover a neck no longer young, not to hide smooth white skin such as that girl possessed.

Julie sold a pair of cuff-links, a marcasite brooch and two tiny gold crosses to a pair of eager schoolgirls, while Mr Gooch and Mr Wexibole took it in turns to go into the inner sanctum with Neville and that girl, and look at goods worth a great deal of money.

Oh, well, she'll be going soon, Julie reminded herself, and then would come an

41

evening with Neville. He would have to be nice to that girl if she was a potential customer, and it really didn't concern Julie.

It seemed a long time before the girl came out. The chauffeur meantime sat in the car reading a newspaper.

At last she emerged, but by then it was almost closing time. Julie noticed with surprise that Neville, walking the girl to the front door, was also dressed for the street, but with his black Homburg and stick and his nice lemon gloves, and he had that remote look again. He called out a general good night that embraced everyone, and Mr Gooch held the door open for them.

Not once by a flicker of an eyelid did Neville indicate that he was aware of Julie's presence. Julie was staggered. He had forgotten all about her. Forgotten the date he had made such a fuss about – that date she herself had at first refused.

Her cheeks scorched as she caught Mr Gooch looking at her.

'Is anything wrong, my dear young lady?'

'Not a thing, thank you,' she said.

'Then you'd better start clearing up ready to go,' he told her.

The business of closing the shop was a ceremony too, at Howe's, but as she wasn't an important member of the staff, and also because of that limp, she was usually shuffled off first. But tonight Mr Gooch's usual kindness was absent. He kept looking at her as she tidied her things away.

And then quite suddenly she was called to the telephone.

Neville Stannard was on the other end of the line, and evidently he hadn't announced himself when his call was taken.

'Julie? Look, my dear – in an awful hurry – got caught up by that customer, I'm afraid. She's important, so I'm having to let you down tonight. Tomorrow, though – all right? Do forgive me.'

'I'm not sure if I can manage tomorrow evening–' she began.

Neville wasn't even listening, and he hung up almost before the words were out of her mouth. Incoherent apologies and good-byes – all in a hurry and rush – but he had done his duty. He had called her to explain, and calmly assumed she would be there waiting for him on the following evening.

She put the receiver down in its cradle and moved away, indignation and disappointment struggling for supremacy in her.

Mr Gooch came over to her at once. 'I would remind you, my dear young lady, that private calls are not allowed.'

Julie felt that this was the last straw for sheer injustice.

She put on her things and left the shop feeling hurt and angry. Why had he asked her out this evening, if he was likely to have an unavoidable engagement with an important customer? Why hadn't he left her alone when she first expressed her reluctance to accept his invitation?

Outside in the street it was noisy with home-going crowds and rush-hour traffic. Julie looked despairingly at the solid wedge of slow-moving vehicles between her and her bus-stop. She would never be able to dodge between them, with this leg of hers. She looked over the traffic to the lights at the end, and saw her bus turn into the street.

Impatience flared up in her. Not so long ago she could have hurried between the vehicles when they came to a momentary halt, and caught the bus that had just edged in to the kerb. Now, having lost it, she would have to wait for twenty minutes.

She decided to walk back to the next stop. It would give her something to do, and it might be easier to cross there.

That was when she became aware of a man following her. It wasn't easy to keep him in sight on the crowded pavement, and it was plain that he sometimes lost her, but never for long.

Once she dodged him by slipping into a shop doorway to wait, and he went by; a man obviously looking for someone. She tried to tell herself that it wasn't her he was wanting, but there was something teasingly familiar about him.

She tried to tell herself not to be idiotic. She was afraid Boyd Markwick would one day track her down, and because of that fear she imagined every man in the street to be him. Did Boyd wear sober clothes like this man, she asked herself? No. Did Boyd ever wear sun-glasses? Never, so far as she recalled. And the day wasn't bright enough to merit them. But people did wear them, through force of habit or in case the sun came out, and it was no reason to think that this was Boyd because of dark glasses. Yet, it was Boyd's height, the way Boyd held his head, the way Boyd walked.

She was shaking all over. If it *were* Boyd, she reasoned, trying to still the excited flutter of her pulse, it must be that he was here by accident. He couldn't *know* she had come to Fleckbury. And she would never be sure whether it were Boyd or not unless the man removed those dark glasses.

But he had gone, lost somewhere in the crowds, so she slipped out, aching to cross that road before the next bus came along. But there he was again, this time coming towards her, and if it were Boyd, he would surely recognise her, meeting her face to face.

Panicking, she again took refuge in a shop doorway, but the man inside thought she was a potential customer and opened the door wide for her, with a beaming smile that was hard to resist. She went inside and stood there, while he closed the door behind her; bemused by the hotchpotch of goods, she just stood and stared.

He was a queer old man. He wore an embroidered velvet waistcoat and a smoking cap with a tassel, and his face was foreign. Dark-skinned, with a hook nose and hooded eyes behind thick lenses. 'You wished for something?' he asked her politely.

'No – yes – well, I'm not sure,' she stammered. Anything to get away from that window. So she walked towards the gloomy back of the shop and pointed to a plate with a relief of a castle, hanging on the wall. 'What is the price of that?'

He got it down for her, and asked her what she thought she should pay for it.

'What is money? I have here many things. Some rare, some just curious. I like people. I like to make customers. Some of my customers come in on a gale of wind, such as you yourself just now – but they come back, again and again. Sometimes they just like to look round, but they always take something away with them. Now, this plaque – do you like it enough to buy it?'

'No. I'll be honest with you. I just came in here to avoid someone. He was searching for me. I can't run any more.'

'It is not a good thing to run away from something … or someone. Always stand and

46

face it out, is what I tell my young friends,' he said with a smile.

He replaced the plaque and picked up a small snuff-box. The top was roughly carved, as if someone had whittled it with a pen-knife. 'This is nice. Ten bob, so you don't go away with nothing. Nine and six, so that makes you a customer.'

She hadn't got nine shillings – or even nine pence – to spare until pay-day. She took the snuff-box from him politely to examine it, wondering how she could possibly say she didn't like it and put it back on the shelf, for it had an undeniable charm, and she could think of a half dozen things it would be useful for, if not for a gift to give someone else.

'You think I rob you? Go on, eight bob and it's yours,' he urged, so for shame's sake she opened her purse, reflecting that she would have to brave the lioness tomorrow, and ask Mrs Leigh for sandwiches, for she wouldn't be able to afford to go out to lunch after this.

And then the shop door opened and a man's bulk filled it, dark against the sudden burst of unexpected sunshine in the street.

A gasp of terror escaped her lips, but as soon as the man moved, she saw that it wasn't the one who had been following her.

He came in with a lazy saunter, shut the door behind him carefully and called cheerfully, 'Is that you, Solly? Can't see you in the gloom back there. Good afternoon to you. Take your time, if you're with a customer. I'm looking for something unusual for my mother. Birthday gift. I'm in no hurry.'

Solly beamed. 'Oh, it's you, Mr Hollidge. I will be with you in a minute,' and he went behind the curtain to find two shillings change for Julie.

The man wandered down the shop and when he came face to face with her, his smile hesitated, then broadened in recognition.

'Hello, you're one of my patients, aren't you? I never forget a face. The name, now – don't tell me–'

'Julie Quinn,' she supplied.

'That's right, Julie Quinn. I remember you especially because you are one of the few patients who didn't respond to my pep talk. I don't believe you even remember me.'

'Oh, yes, I *do*, Mr Hollidge,' Julie said, feeling so relieved that he wasn't the man she had feared, that she was prepared to listen to a hundred pep talks at this moment.

And then, dark against the window, peering in from outside, was that man who had been following her. And as she looked down the length of the shop she knew, deep inside her, that it was indeed Boyd Markwick, and that he knew she was there.

CHAPTER THREE

'What's the matter?' Adam Hollidge asked her and followed her glance.

Solly came out with the change. 'What is it?' He, too, was aware of how agitated she looked.

'That man. He's been following me,' she said faintly.

'So that is why you come in here,' Solly observed. 'Not to worry. I get rid of him,' and he went puffing down the shop and opened the door.

'That is a nice picture, very nice. You wish to come in and inspect it?' he invited.

Julie watched Boyd hesitate, then make a protesting movement of the hand, before he moved off.

Solly came back chuckling.

'That is the way to find out if they want to buy something,' he said. 'Now, you come again. If you have no cash, what does it matter? You come to see old Solly and tell him your troubles. Any friend of Mr Hollidge is a friend of old Solly.'

'I'm not a friend of his, just a patient,' Julie explained, with meticulous truth Adam Hollidge found amusing.

'We'll see about that. I'll come back later and look for that small thing,' he told Solly. 'No hurry at all. Meanwhile I can't let a patient loose in the High Street in this state,' and he took the protesting Julie out of the shop.

'Really, I can manage,' she said. Everyone seemed to want to take her home, as if she were helpless.

'Tell me about this man,' Adam Hollidge said.

They were no longer in the High Street. Alleys, blocked by old-fashioned stone posts, were a feature of Fleckbury. He took her through this one as if he knew his way. It led to a car park and when he had settled her beside him he drove out of the back way, so that if Boyd were lurking near the shop waiting for her, he would have lost her completely.

'He's my cousin,' she said.

'Go on.'

'He was with me in the accident.'

This really interested Adam Hollidge. So far, she had been as reticent with the doctors at the hospital, about what had happened to her leg, as she had been with Neville Stannard. Brief details were on her card that had been transferred with her from her old hospital, but Adam Hollidge felt that if he persevered while she was in this mood, he might well get the personal angle – a thing which most patients were reluctant to include.

'Look here, do you very much mind if we don't go to your home at once? I haven't had anything to eat for hours, and I'm sure you could do with some food – or will it put your family out?'

'I haven't got a family, and anyway, my landlady wasn't expecting me. I've just remembered that. I had a date only it fell through.'

'Bad luck. Then I suggest we go and talk somewhere. I have an absorbing interest in patients who get sent on to me from other hospitals with a carry-on-as-before comment on the bottom of the notes. I do like to feel that I can prove the other chaps were wrong and that I might be able to effect a cure, or at least an improvement. After all, someone fresh coming to the problem, might see it in a new light. Eh?'

He smiled so confidentially at her that it made her feel warm inside, wanted.

She studied his face covertly. It was not a face that one could describe. She had been right about that – she still couldn't improve on the description of him that she had given to Mrs Leigh. But his voice was so nice and he was so friendly.

She waited for him to slow down when they approached the Carlton Hotel. Everyone seemed to think that the Carlton was the last word in good food and service in this district, but apparently Adam Hollidge didn't share this idea.

He kept driving and remarked, 'I don't really think that Fleckbury has a lot to offer, and Eltonstock is merely the place where I work. I do like a change of scene when I'm off duty. Now, in Chagwell Green there is an inn called "The Jolly Blacksmith", where they do really excellent roast chicken and two vegetables. How does that appeal?'

She looked so small and frail, sitting neatly beside him, but there was such an abundance of interest in that little face. It lit at one moment, then as quickly drained of enthusiasm. She teetered between moods like quicksilver and it all showed in her face.

'The Jolly Blacksmith' was not in the village centre. It lay at the bottom of a narrow street, with the river splashing over stones at the end. There was a door that led over a narrow footbridge to an island in the river.

'Part of the inn's property. Nice to sit there and drink cider on a hot evening,' Adam Hollidge told her. 'But for this evening, I think a nice corner table in here would meet the circumstances.'

He knew his way around. He waved to a pink-faced man behind the bar, and went through. A jolly woman with a lot of black hair piled on the top of her head in stiff coils, called out to him by name and asked if he wanted the usual and he said he did.

It was a long, narrow, low-ceilinged room with small oak tables and wheel-back chairs. Bits of brass and pewter hung from blackened rafters, and the windows were small casement ones with diamond shaped panes. Cosy, yet very clean. Julie felt she was going to enjoy this much more than being out with Neville Stannard.

'Do you bring all your new patients here, Mr Hollidge?'

'Never,' he said stoutly. 'But you see, they don't all run to hide in Solly's shop. Practically never, I would say.'

That made her laugh. She had a pretty laugh, which brought a deep cleft to one side of her cheek, and her eyes momentarily danced with fun. She must have been very pretty once. She wasn't at all unattractive now, he thought, in spite of that scar. It showed now, because the wind had blown her fringe away. As if sensing that it was uncovered, she put up a nervous hand to rearrange her hair, and the smile died.

'Don't feel so badly about it,' he couldn't resist saying. 'You ought to see some of my patients. You know something can be done about that scar, of course? Plastic surgery is a wonderful thing, and taken for granted nowadays.'

The food came. After the chicken, fruit salad and cream, and all the time he gently drew her out to talk, not only of the past she had left behind when she had come to Fleckbury but her tastes, and the life she was leading now. To her intense surprise, she didn't mind talking to him. He didn't really seem like a stranger.

'I'd got settled in that bookshop. Reuben Floy was a dear, and he taught me an awful lot, and I liked his sister, too. But all the time Boyd was in the background.'

'He is the only relative you have now?'

'I said he was a cousin, didn't I? He's only a cousin by marriage actually, but he featured so much in my childhood, I suppose I forget that he isn't really a blood relative at all. He makes claims on me as if he were.'

'What sort of claims?'

'Sometimes a promise to say I had him with me a whole evening or a whole day or just a specified number of hours. Things like that. Sometimes he used to ask me to go with him to visit people, instead of taking a girl friend. He would never tell me clearly what it was all about. Just vague explanations. Business deals. I never got the clear facts out of him. And I lent him money sometimes. Oh, he always paid it back again sooner or later, but he borrowed it again so soon that in the end we didn't really know which loan he was settling. It's always been like that.'

'What does he do for a living?'

Julie wrinkled her forehead. 'You know, this may sound queer, but I don't really know. He changes jobs frequently, and they're always the sort of jobs that depend on personality rather than training. As a boy, he had the reputation of being able to talk his way in or out of anything, and when he grew up he said he could make a living out of it, though I thought at the time it was a joke. But now I'm not so sure.'

'Because now it's no joke,' Adam Hollidge observed shrewdly.

'Because now it's no joke,' she agreed. 'That last time he wanted me to pick him up in the car I was driving. It wasn't my car.'

His eyebrows raised, so Julie hastened to explain. 'I had to pick up my employer from the station sometimes, or drive him there. This was a time when I had taken him to the station for an evening appointment, and I had agreed to give Boyd a lift on the way back.'

'In your employer's car?'

She shrugged. 'At first I'd said no. I don't know why, because I'd given him lifts before. There hadn't seemed any harm in it. But I had a queer feeling, that I'd never had about it before. In the end I gave in, though, and said I'd pick Boyd up just once more.'

'Go on.'

'There was a mews at the back of the bookshop. For the sake of convenience I used to park the car there, go to my digs for the evening and then drive back to the station.

She frowned, and halted, memories crowding in. Adam Hollidge gently prodded her back to the story by prompting, 'You were a chauffeuse?'

She watched him top her glass with white wine, then hastily looked up, denying that last suggestion about her job. 'No, not a chauffeuse at all. A sort of secretary to the store manager. Well, not properly that – only part time. Part of the time I served behind the jewellery counter. Well, in a store like that, it was merely costume jewellery. I didn't like the job much.'

'Yet you're doing much the same sort of work now.'

'Oh, no. This is a proper jeweller's – Howe's. Nothing unorthodox about that. But at the old job nothing was really official about it, and to tell the truth, it wasn't very comfortable. The store manager made a favourite of me. He was showing signs of wanting to be more than friendly and I didn't quite know what to do about it, short of leaving. He was an odd man. Nice enough to me up to a point. But he'd sacked his chauffeur, so when he discovered I could drive, he said he'd like me to drive him sometimes, and there it was. I agreed. I didn't see how I could get out of it.'

'Didn't he drive himself?'

'No. There was some sort of rumour that he'd been in a crash and lost his nerve– I never found out the exact details. I think he knew I sometimes gave a lift to Boyd but he never said anything.'

She sipped her wine, bracing herself.

'Well, that night Boyd was in an odd mood. He telephoned me and said he was in a spot of bother. It worried me.'

'And then?'

She hesitated on the brink of further confidences. 'Honestly, I don't know why I'm telling you all this. I never have told anyone else. Are you going to put it down in the hospital records? I suppose I ran that risk when I started.'

'You haven't told me anything very dreadful yet,' he said, smiling. 'But I won't let you go any further, if you'd rather I didn't. I do want to know everything. I wish you'd trust me.'

'Why do you want to know about me?'

'I want to decide in my own mind what is the actual effect of all that has happened at the time of the accident, on yourself – and I can't do that without having the complete picture. I know you are afraid of running into this Boyd person again. I know that you ran away from your old home to come here to work and now he's found you (or so you think), you appear to be prepared for flight again. I hope you won't be tempted to do anything so foolish.'

'If you knew what Boyd's name means – he just brings trouble. He terrifies me.'

'But I feel bound to point out that you don't know for certain that it was your cousin you saw. You admitted that yourself. You didn't get close enough to him to be sure. So until you are sure, I beg of you not to start running again. Meanwhile, finish the story, then we'll see what can be done.'

'Boyd wanted me to meet him at Cockle Way. That's a sort of road that runs much higher than the one he was to be on. His road went under a railway bridge. He said he'd come up the steps by the side of the bridge and nip into my car.'

'What was all this for?'

'I found out afterwards that it was to throw off some friends of his in another car. He didn't say at the time that he would be on the back of a motor-bike or that he was going to ask his friend to ditch it and hide. I don't know what went wrong – I suppose his friend didn't have time to carry out those instructions or perhaps there were people about – anyway, he just kept on, which was the cause of the trouble later.'

'Was this all serious or was it all a kind of a game?'

'Oh, no, Mr Hollidge, it was no game. It was serious all right. So serious, I can't get out of my mind's eye the picture of Boyd tearing up those steps and looking over his shoulder at a car just turning the corner into the street below. It wasn't like Boyd. I was so uneasy, I asked him what was happening. He wrenched the door open, leapt in, shut it and shouted at me to drive on.'

She drank a little of the wine, her eyes dark and brooding. 'He said he'd explain later. He kept giving me directions. We seemed to be weaving about, up this street and down that. He kept looking behind, and I was so worried, I took a wrong turning and landed us in a dead end. He was so angry, and it cost us time backing out.'

'Your cousin Boyd doesn't sound at all a reasonable person.'

She shook her head slightly. 'In the end he said I was to drive the car back to the yard behind the bookshop and he'd cut through the back and take a taxi, which should throw his friends off the scent. He said not to worry – he'd made one of them angry but it'd be all right when the man had cooled down.'

'But weren't you surprised at this fantastic way of going on? I find this all very reprehensible,' Adam Hollidge exploded. 'Anyway, continue with the story. Did you drive back to the yard?'

'Yes, but there was a van creeping out. It was totally unexpected. I'd almost turned to go in. Boyd yelled and grabbed the wheel.'

'The young fool.'

59

'I kept my head and straightened the car, though. The only thing I could do on the split second was to drive past the bookshop and out at the other end. But that was blocked by things coming in. His friend on the motor-bike had thought of the yard behind the shop too, and he was coming in straight at us, and fast. I remember braking and making a lot of noise. It all happened so quickly then– I couldn't back, because that van was behind us, and there was a car behind the motor-bike, and my car was running into a skid.'

'Good heavens!'

'I couldn't stop it, and the street was so narrow and – this is the really awful part, and it keeps me awake at night – Reuben Floy ran out, straight under the wheels.'

She broke off, covering her face with her hands.

'Steady, steady,' Adam urged, and signalled the waiter for something stronger than the white wine.

'I couldn't stop the car,' she said again. 'He must have come out to see what was going on, but the street was so narrow! I hit him, then the car overturned.'

'Drink this,' Adam Hollidge said, forcing the glass to her lips.

'I couldn't do a thing about it,' she kept saying, over and over again. 'I wanted to get out and see what had happened to Reuben,

60

only I couldn't move. I kept trying and I think I must have kept blacking out. It was like a nightmare. All that noise and I couldn't move, I couldn't.'

'No, no, I appreciate that. Drink some more of this.'

On his notes at the hospital, all he had about the accident was the terse comment: 'Patient driving car which ran into skid and overturned, pinning leg. Some delay before being able to release patient from damaged car.'

'What happened to your cousin?' he said presently, when her teeth had stopped chattering.

'I don't know. I didn't see him again until … today. That's if it's him. They thought I was alone in the car. He must have got out somehow without being seen and gone through the bookshop. I don't know; I wanted to see if I could help Reuben, only I never saw him again either, and the bookshop was sold up, and I tried to contact his sister, only she wouldn't answer my letters.'

She had to stop talking because Adam was forcing more spirit to her lips. It scorched her throat, but she felt better. She stopped shaking, but she was still back in the past, he could see. 'All that noise…' she said again, and as a last comment, 'And now Boyd's back again.'

'But you don't know that for certain,'

Adam urged. 'You saw someone you thought looked like him, but dark glasses change people so. You just can't be certain.'

That comforted her a little.

'Let's go,' he said, and took her out of the inn.

Beyond Chagwell Green was Chagwell Heights. There was a lake, an incredibly peaceful place in the fading light. Massed trees went down to the shores on one side. One small sailboat blew about in the middle of the empty sheet of water. It was all very pleasant. Julie visibly eased out.

'I like this,' she murmured.

'Do you sail?' Adam asked her. He leaned back, opened all the windows, and turned to study her.

'No. I've never had the chance. Do you sail?'

'Sometimes. One must escape from one's work occasionally, and sailing is a complete escape.'

'Don't you like your work?' she asked him, glad to talk of something else. Her past had been too uncomfortable a subject.

'Very much. So much so that I find I get involved with my patients, to their irritation.' He smiled broadly. 'They rarely understand that I can't just wave a magic wand over them and cure them, without knowing all about their lives, what's worrying them, what pleases them, how other people and events affect them. And what could replace the thing they've lost.'

'Lost?' The word seemed to startle her.

'Yes. People, by the very nature of things, must lose or replace. That's life. If it isn't a limb in question, or one of the senses, it could be a job that's lost, or a home; a pattern of life, a source of income. They need help to set about replacing that thing, and the quicker it is replaced, the quicker the cure. Now take you, for instance.'

'Oh, must we? Haven't we talked enough about me? I feel awfully guilty at taking up so much of your time. It was more than good of you to come to my rescue and to take me out to eat, but I really feel I've imposed on your kindness enough.'

'I hadn't anything else to do,' he said mildly.

'What about your mother? I heard you asking for a suitable gift for her.'

'My mother is a sensible woman. She expects me when she sees me and she doesn't panic if I don't arrive.'

'Even so, you must have had something else you wanted to do, instead of getting stuck with a patient out of hospital hours.'

'On the contrary, you interest me. I hate being defeated by the course of things. Just because everyone else has said you won't be able to do much about that leg, doesn't mean that I have to agree. To that end, I want you to cut down the hours of standing on it.'

'Oh, but I can't do that. I need that job.'

'I know that. And I understand how you feel about the claustrophobic tendencies. That isn't surprising after your ordeal when you were trapped in the overturned car. But I would suggest asking your firm to allow you to work mornings only, and find other work in the afternoons.'

'That may not be so easy,' she said, looking worried.

'Is it the financial aspect?' he asked her gently. 'Well, I think I might help there. There is clerical work to be done in the hospital, for instance, and we can never get enough part-timers.'

'But it's Eltonstock – that journey,' she protested.

'I know. I'm thinking about it. Something could be arranged.'

'You make it all sound so easy,' she said.

'Half the things one thinks of as difficult, aren't nearly so hard in the eyes of another person,' he told her quietly.

'You're fixing everything for me,' she said. 'Why are you? I'm only too grateful, but I would like to know why you bother.'

'Let's say I've got that sort of disposition. I like fixing things for people. Mind you, it isn't every patient who cares for it. There are some patients who tell the poor old doctor quite frankly to stop his meddling.'

'Oh, I wouldn't do that,' she said, faintly shocked, until she saw that he was smiling broadly again. 'So long as you can assure me that you're not going to a lot of trouble, and that you'd do it for everyone else as well—'

He was serious all at once. 'Not quite, Julie,' he said, after a pause. 'Let's say that mine is a very lonely life, and I have a personal interest in a selected few patients that helps to combat the loneliness. I sometimes like to be friends with a patient. There's an old fellow who lives over a shop down by the wharves in Eltonstock – you know those narrow twisting streets? His trade is going from door to door mending mats – at least, it was, before he got injured in a crane accident. He's a very interesting old man. I go to his place sometimes to play backgammon with him.'

Julie listened, her eyes wide, imagining the old man with the guard on his thumb, sitting on the doorstep stitching a new edge to the rough matting. She had seen such people. How could such a man as this, mix with Adam Hollidge?

'He was a seafaring man, years ago,' Adam went on; 'a very interesting old fellow, Isaac Jones.'

He glanced at her with a smile. 'And then there's Eva Yanova. She wanted to be a top-line ballet dancer. Odd thing, it's always the treasured limb that gets hurt. Nowadays she propels herself at top rate in a chair, and she makes a fair living designing costumes for the stage. We're great friends. And I'd like to be friends with you, Julie, and help you, if you will accept it in the spirit in which I intend it, and don't get prickly about independence and favours and such things.'

'How did you know—?' she began, and then she laughed. 'I suppose it sticks out a mile.'

'It does,' he agreed, laughing. 'I've been watching you. I could almost hear the arguments for and against, going on in that head of yours. Will you have my friendship?'

'I'd be glad to,' she said simply.

They shook hands on it.

Darkness was falling fast now. The sailboat had long since reached the shore, and its owner had lovingly done those things to it that made it ready for the night. Now there was nothing left to ruffle the surface of the lake. Subconsciously Julie had been watching the sail being run down, the mast being folded, the little craft being eased on to its trolley and run ashore into the boathouse that looked rather like a gay-painted toy. The owner and his dog, two small specks now on the far edge of the water, were merging into the dusk. No one left, only herself and this man who had edged his way into her life with his comforting voice, his firm promise of friendship; a man who, whether he knew it or not, would inevitably be called on to form a buffer between her and the old life which, instinct told her, was pressing hard to reach out and grasp at her, pull her back.

CHAPTER FOUR

Adam Hollidge promised Julie that he would approach the firm of Howe's the Jeweller, for her, and re-arrange her working hours. He said it in such a friendly way that it never occurred to her that this wasn't the best way out; she felt comfortable, warm inside, for the first time since the accident. Someone was taking a personal interest in her, looking after her.

Yet she didn't mention it at her lodgings. Vera Leigh was inclined to be short-tempered, and by the time Julie had heard the full recital of Vera's disappointing evening at the Church Hall, it didn't seem the time or the place to relate what had been happening to herself. So Julie sat over her cocoa and biscuits in the kitchen, just listening, and looking sympathetic, and reflecting that she was rather glad that circumstances made it possible for her to keep Adam's offer of friendship to herself, like a warm-hugged secret.

Gideon sat silent, too, throwing in a propitiating word now and again to his wife, and getting roundly scolded for his efforts. Julie would have liked to tell Gideon about Adam Hollidge's kindness, and his offer to cut short her working hours for her, but there was little opportunity, for Vera hustled them both to their bedrooms early.

Long after Julie had gone upstairs, she could hear Vera banging about in the kitchen, and she wondered whether Gideon had smuggled some of his gardening magazines down from the attic to read in bed until his wife came upstairs.

Somehow Adam Hollidge's friendship had made Julie feel so secure that she forgot about the need to keep an eye open for that young man who had been following her. She was even persuaded that she had made a mistake, and that that man had not been following her at all, but had been looking for someone else.

It was busy at the shop. Even Howe's the Jeweller was affected by the Saturday trade. Julie felt really tired by the time she was free to go to lunch.

Today she had sandwiches and intended to take them to the park nearby, to eat with a bottled fizzy drink and a straw.

It was a crisp, sunny day, and Fleckbury looked inviting.

As Julie left the shop, Neville Stannard came out behind her and took her arm, walking by her side.

'Julie, I'm terribly sorry about last night,' he said.

'Please don't mention it,' she replied, trying not to sound cool. He had been in the inner sanctum all the morning, and when he had gone through the shop to go out for his coffee, he had had Mr Gooch with him and he hadn't even glanced Julie's way.

'You're cross with me, and I don't wonder. It must have looked awful, but Julie, what could I do? You realise who that girl is, of course?'

Julie shook her head. She didn't know who the girl was, and she wasn't particularly interested, but it was certain that Neville was going to tell her.

'She's Dian Ackery.'

It wasn't possible to pretend that she didn't know that name, Julie thought crossly. It was only amazing to her now, that she hadn't realised who that girl was when she came into the shop. She had seen her picture in the newspapers. Dian Ackery, the daughter of Jerrett Ackery. If possible, Julie knew more about the father.

Jerrett Ackery had made his money in the Watchford Cement Works, she now recalled, but he wasn't known so much for that; his name was linked with local charities, and people remembered him because he was so rich. He had a yacht, a town house and a country mansion, and Dian, on the strength of that, thrust her way in everywhere.

People who had no money amused themselves by wondering how much the Ackery family really had, and how they had made it all. Vera Leigh was fond of saying she didn't know for certain but she had heard it rumoured that he had a chain of night clubs in London and one-armed bandit joints. Vera said this with a certain amount of relish, but Julie didn't believe it. That sort of rumour was always to be found floating around a small town like Fleckbury, and a little shiver went through Julie. Suppose Boyd did come here? What sort of rumours would start up about him?

'She's very important in this town,' Neville continued earnestly, 'and her father is an extremely good customer of the firm.'

'Then of course you had to escort Miss Ackery, so please don't think any more about it,' Julie said.

'But I do think a lot about it, m'dear. I'm fed up at having to stand you up like that, and I want to make amends for it. I've got something very nice lined up for tonight, and I've got permission for you to go off early and get prettied up.'

'I'm sorry,' she said, bright spots of colour in her cheeks. 'I'm going out with a friend tonight. I didn't know you'd want to take me.'

'Well, for goodness sake, explain to your pal what happened, Julie – she'll understand. Break the date, my dear, I've booked seats.'

'You don't understand. It isn't a girl, and I wouldn't want to break a date with anyone.'

'I thought you said you had no friends in this town?' he asked, looking frankly surprised.

'That was so, when you asked me.'

'And you've got yourself dated up in jolly quick time, eh? Oh, well, good for you. I wouldn't have thought you were such a fast worker, Julie.'

She was angry. 'It isn't like that. It's just a friend, but he has been very kind to me, and I just don't feel like breaking the date. If you want to know, he was kind to me when he found I'd been stood up last evening, so I'm sure I wouldn't want to let him down at the last minute.'

For a second she thought Neville was going to be furious. Then all of a sudden he started to laugh. *'Touché,'* he said, sketching a salute at her. 'And I hope you never stand me up in favour of someone else, just to get your own back.'

There wasn't any reason why he couldn't have dated her up for one night the following week, but he said nothing about that.

She supposed he had happened to have that one evening free and thought she'd be ready to jump at the chance. She didn't care to be taken for granted in that way, and even though he had been kind to her on that first occasion, it had, she recalled, been a rather overbearing kindness, and she couldn't forget the arrogant way he had had of standing staring at her in the shop during her first week there. Anyway, he could have let her know sooner, about last night.

No, it was all wrong. She shouldn't have let him take her to that first lunch, she thought, as she watched him stride off among the traffic, back, presumably, to where he had left his car parked.

She ate a tranquil lunch by herself in the park, thinking about Adam Hollidge, but the memory of that man whom she had mistakenly thought was Boyd intruded itself, because that was the way she had first met Adam, and the memory would always go hand in hand with the less pleasant one of the man outside the shop window. What, she asked herself, had made her so certain it was Boyd? Fear, because she knew in her heart that he would find her one day? Or had there been something about him, some little thing, that had reminded her of Boyd?

And even as she sat there, thinking about him, there he was, on the other side of the lake.

The dark glasses were still there, and the sober good tailoring, but now she knew how she had managed to recognise him in spite of these things which amounted almost to a disguise. It was his walk, that self-confident rather jaunty swagger, and the set of his head. You could draw a straight line down the back of his neck from the crown of his head, and there was only one word to describe him under the charm: cocky.

She put the rest of her lunch away, her appetite gone. Somehow she must get out of the park before he came round the lake to where she was.

If he hadn't seen her, and kept walking round the edge of the lake, she might have a chance, but of course, he had seen her.

He took a short cut over the narrow bridge where people stood watching the children's paddle boats going underneath. Before she had limped more than a few yards, he was there at her side.

'Julie,' he said. Just like that. Low, half-laughing. A voice pitched to charm. The voice he used on other girls. He had no need to use it on her, she thought resentfully. He hadn't used it on her, that last time, when he had shouted directions and finally caused her to crash her employer's car.

The memory of all that made her turn on him and almost moan, 'Why don't you leave me alone, Boyd?'

'Now there's a way to greet me, after I've gone to such trouble to find you, Julie. Why didn't you get in touch? You knew where I'd be.'

'Because I wanted nothing more to do with you,' she said heatedly.

'You're still cross with me about that car,' he said. 'But the owner wasn't terribly cross. Not with me, anyway. He was rather peeved about you giving lifts to your boyfriends.'

'How do you know?'

'Because I took the trouble to telephone him to find out. Oh, I didn't say I was your cousin; I'm not so foolish. I let him think I was a reporter, and how he talked. Rather heartless, I felt, considering the way he ran you around, doing the old chauffeur act when you ought to have been off duty.'

'You were glad of it – glad of the chance of a lift.'

'Yes, well, never mind that. I'm sure you'd like to know how I found you. I discovered you'd been in hospital. Why didn't you jump clear when you felt the car swerve, you little idiot? I did– I jumped clear and hopped it through the bookshop.'

'I guessed as much. I couldn't jump clear. I was pinned underneath. So now you know. What do you want me for, Boyd? I haven't got any money to lend you.'

'Now is that nice? Who said I wanted money from you? I'm pretty comfortable at the moment – at least, I shall be, if this little idea of mine comes up.'

'Oh, no, Boyd, not again,' she said, with more decision in her voice than she realised.

'Now who said I wanted help from you?'

'No, Boyd, stop pretending to be surprised – you know you always come to me with your brilliant ideas and try to drag me into trouble with you. Well, I've been a fool before, but never again. Never again.'

'Now Julie, love, this is not nice. It wasn't my fault that you were such a rotten driver. I tell you, I got a bad shock when I eventually traced you to the hospital and heard what had happened to you, but it seems you got transferred to a hospital at Eltonstock – dreary place, isn't it? Might a poor cousin ask why you chose that place?'

'It isn't your business, Boyd.'

'But it is, love, it is. You got in a mess through being kind to me so now I must be kind to you and that's just what I mean to be. I've got a room in the town, so as to be near you, and a car of sorts – not a very smart one but it's lent by a friend and beggars can't be choosers – and I'm going to take you for some jolly rides and we'll talk over old times.'

'You don't even think it necessary to ask if I want you to take me out or whether there's anyone else,' she asked him.

He laughed softly. 'So what? So you've got

a little friend, but I can share my cousin with her pals, surely? And that's what I'm going to do. I believe you work in Howe's the Jeweller,' he said, in an altered tone, carefully studying his nails.

'So that's it,' she said, in a low, unhappy voice.

'Don't be so silly, jumping to unkind conclusions. That isn't it at all,' he said, in a pained voice. 'My wild days are over, I do assure you. I just wanted to check where you worked, in order to pick you up in the car and run you home.'

'I'm not going home. I'm being taken out tonight by a friend. So you won't need to collect me from work. But Boyd, since you are here, just what was that all about – that mad chase, the day I crashed the car?'

'I told you, love – a business friend got cross with me. We made it up afterwards and it's all right now.'

He was so smilingly casual about it, that she didn't know whether to believe him or not. 'And you robbed me of the use of one leg, you left me trapped and bleeding in the wreck of that car, you did this to my face,' she said, slowly, pulling her fringe aside to show him the scar, 'just because a friend of yours was cross with you?'

Boyd didn't like scars or details of injuries. He blanched. 'I say, old love, I'm terribly sorry. Truly I am. I hadn't a clue. Still, they can do things with the jolly old plastic surgery, can't they? Work wonders nowadays, they tell me. As to the way you walk, I assure you, I hardly noticed it. No, absolutely not. Don't think another thing about it.'

'It's all very well, Boyd–' she began.

'As to tonight,' he broke in hastily. 'Well, I understand, love. I'll drop into the shop on Monday and take you out for a bite to eat.'

'Won't you understand, Boyd – *I don't want you to.*'

'Oh, rot. You'll feel different on Monday,' he told her. 'Once you've had a chance to get used to the thought of old Boyd around again, you'll be all right. Believe me, you'll be glad to see your cheery old cousin squiring you again just as it used to be.'

Just as it used to be. She was shaking all over by the time she reached the shop. It hadn't been so bad a meeting as she had feared, but knowing Boyd, that wasn't the half of it. He might well have a source of income, but that didn't mean he hadn't got one of those schemes of his lined up to include her, and that was what she was particularly anxious to avoid.

When she got back to the shop, she found that Adam Hollidge had already kept his promise and contacted the firm.

Mr Gooch called her into the inner office. 'Why didn't you say that you were finding it difficult to carry on your duties because of your injured leg, young lady?'

'It doesn't bother me, Mr Gooch, and I wasn't going to do anything about it. It's the hospital people who want me to do less standing. I do hope it won't inconvenience anyone.'

She stood there with her fingers crossed behind her back, hoping Mr Gooch wouldn't say that they had no room for part-timers. But in Fleckbury it wasn't easy to get good assistants and Mr Gooch knew that Julie was a favourite with the customers and staff already. She was quiet and patient, and had a flair for appearing really interested in the customer's needs. In any case it wasn't entirely for him to say that this or that member of the staff should be dismissed for such a reason. Howe's the Jewellers prided themselves on their initial choice of employees and boasted that they were never wrong in their judgement and therefore never had to dismiss anyone.

Julie didn't know this and wished that Adam Hollidge hadn't been so quick off the mark. Mr Gooch said he thought he might put in a good word for her to keep her on as part-time, but he added that he felt next week was too early to start the new arrangement.

Her surprise was evident. She hadn't expected that Adam Hollidge would want her to give up all-day standing so soon.

She went back to her counter in some bewilderment. Did this mean that her leg wasn't as reliable as she had thought it would be? Or did it indicate that Adam Hollidge thought he could see the chance of a cure and was paving the way?

She needed some assurance about this so passionately and he had spoken as if he thought his colleagues might have been wrong about the likelihood of a permanent limp.

She didn't see Neville Stannard any more that day, and she was very glad when she at last left the shop and found Adam waiting for her.

He seemed so solid, not the type of man to be nice one day and let a person down the next. She settled in the car with him, feeling that at last it was going to be all right, until she remembered her encounter with Boyd in the park in the lunch hour.

'It was him,' she said, coming right out with it. 'I thought it was Boyd. And it was. There's something about the way he walks.' She glanced quickly at Adam. 'He caught me up in the park and I couldn't get away. You weren't there to rescue me.'

'What happened? Did it upset you?' he asked tautly.

'No. It wasn't too bad actually. I felt shaken, of course, because I'd dreaded meeting him again. He said I was silly and that all he wanted to do was to make amends for everything.'

'What does that mean?'

'Oh, for always borrowing money from me and expecting me to do exactly what he wanted. Do you know, I think he really means what he says, this time. Well, he hasn't asked me for money and he seems so reasonable.'

'Where is he staying?'

'He says he's got a room, near my digs. I wish he hadn't found out where I lived. He wanted to take me out tonight. I was so glad I could say I was going out with someone else.'

'Is that the only reason you're glad to be with me?' he asked, with a lop-sided smile. She looked so startled that he said hastily, 'Only teasing, to try and reassure you.'

'Oh. Oh, well, you don't have to worry. I'm not quite sure of him, of course, but I don't think I have any real need for alarm this time. I'll tell you if I have, may I?'

'Of course. I want you to. I told you, didn't I, that your welfare concerns me closely? Speaking of that, has anyone at your shop mentioned that I've tackled them about your job, Julie?'

'Oh, yes, indeed they have,' she said wryly. 'Old Mr Gooch wanted to know why I hadn't given them warning about it earlier. He was cross that it was to start on Monday.

Does it have to be so soon?'

'Of course. If they make any more fuss, leave the place altogether. I can fix you up in another job. But I don't think you'll find they will make a real fuss. That old man is a pest – he wouldn't let me begin to explain, over the telephone. It isn't as if he doesn't know me. I've been in there before for many gifts for my mother and aunts. That's Howe's all over – make a fuss on principle.'

He said it sweepingly, yet his manner, as always, made her feel that everything was all right, and she was content to leave it to him.

It was the first of many evenings spent with him. The pattern went with someone – not necessarily Adam but anyone who happened to be near Canary Lane – picking Julie up in the morning for her work at the hospital. Someone took her back to Fleckbury for lunch and her work in the shop, and then Adam would pick her up in the evening. It was to be as simple as that, and for the first week it worked out that way, until Neville Stannard took notice of her again.

'What's going on, Julie? I asked you about that leg of yours and you said it didn't worry you. Now old Gooch says the hospital is stirring things up and won't let you work with us in the mornings.'

'I know, and I'm sorry, but I didn't think they were going to be so quick about arranging things but they did have an opening in

81

the office and it's sitting down most of the time.'

'Whose idea was it?' he asked searchingly.

She had just been brought back to Fleckbury, having had lunch in the hospital's canteen. She stopped talking to Neville to show a customer some little brooches, but he didn't walk away. He stayed watching her, very much with that old manner of his; staring, those light blue eyes of his boring through her. She wished he would go away.

After the customer had gone, he returned to the attack. 'I've been away this last week,' he said. 'I was astonished to find when I came back that new arrangements had been made about you.'

'Did you have a nice holiday?' she asked.

'What? I haven't been on holiday. I've been away on business for the firm.'

'But what would a store detective—?' she began, but his elevated eyebrows somehow didn't encourage the direct question.

'We'd better discuss this off the premises,' he said in a nettled tone as another customer came up.

He took her out to tea at a nearby restaurant. There wasn't any real reason why she should refuse to go, but it was the odd way he did it. He said to Mr Gooch, 'I want to discuss something with Miss Quinn. You won't mind if I take her out to tea?'

Mr Gooch shook his head. 'No, Mr

Stannard, of course not.'

Julie hastily washed her hands and gathered her bag and gloves. As she followed Neville out of the shop, she said, 'He doesn't seem to mind what you do, does he?'

'Should he?' Neville retorted, with such an arrogant air that she was abashed. All her former dislike for him rushed back to her and she said, 'What did you want to talk to me about that couldn't be said in the shop?'

He waited until they were seated at their table before he answered that. 'I have the feeling, Julie, that just because of that unfortunate affair of the customer and the broken date, you have finished with me.'

'Can't we forget all about it? It isn't really important, is it?' she said uncomfortably.

'It is, to me. Isn't it, to you?'

'I agree with Mr Gooch, actually. He went to a lot of pains to make me see that friendship with you was unsuitable. That was when you telephoned to say you had had to take a customer out. He was very cross and told me I wasn't to have private calls.'

That seemed to amuse him. 'And it was me on the line? Oh, how unjust. Why didn't you say who it was?'

'He didn't really give me a chance, and anyway, what good would it have done?'

'You don't think much of me, do you, Julie? Your frankness is so refreshing. You really are a delightful little person. Come on, let's make it up and be friends again.'

'But there isn't anything to make up, is there?'

He shrugged. 'All right, we'll leave it for the moment. Now, tell me about this little job you're doing at the hospital. What are they paying you for it?'

'Really, I wish you wouldn't trouble about me so, Mr Stannard,' she protested.

'That means, I suppose, how can it possibly concern me. Well, it does, you know – very much. Do you know what I'm going to do? I'm going to get you on full pay even though you only work part-time for us. Yes, I am – and I'm not taking any notice of any protests from you, young woman. I think you're worth full pay. I've watched you handling the customers. I like your manner. And I'm hoping that when your leg's finished troubling you, you'll come back to us full time.'

She was very uncomfortable. 'Please, Mr Stannard, I must ask you to leave things alone. One of the surgeons at the hospital has arranged everything. He's looking after me, and he'll think it very odd if someone else tries to do something different.'

'Oh, it's one of the hospital chaps you're interested in, is it? Why didn't you say so? Is he the one who's been taking you out every evening? What happened to the chap with the dark glasses who's been hanging about outside the shop?'

84

'Has he?' Julie whispered. 'When? How do you know?'

'Now what's the matter? You've gone white as a sheet,' he drawled. 'Is your love life in such a tangle, Julie? I thought you were insisting not so long ago that you didn't know a soul. Not the truth, was it?'

'When has someone been hanging about the shop with dark glasses?' she asked again.

'Oh, have a heart – I was just joking. I saw him today. The chap asked me if you worked there and if you were going to be long, and I confess I had a great deal of pleasure in telling him that I didn't know what he was talking about.'

'Why did you do that?'

'It may have escaped your notice that I'm interested in you enough to want to take you around. Now, when are you going to consent to make another date with me?'

CHAPTER FIVE

That night Adam Hollidge wasn't free to see her. Julie's disappointment was crushing.

Mr Gooch looked disapprovingly at her but this time he didn't dare to tell her not to take private calls. Neville Stannard was in the office with him.

He followed Julie outside. 'Are you free tonight, then?' Neville asked in a low tone that Mr Gooch couldn't possibly have heard.

She didn't like him and she didn't want to go out with him but she didn't want to make an enemy of him, so she said, 'Not really. The man with the dark glasses is my cousin, if you want to know, and he did say he'd be calling – he isn't in Fleckbury for very long. I ought to let him know I shall be at home.'

'I think that's an excuse. I'm going to drive you home and find out,' Neville said.

Mr Gooch called her back into the office when Neville left her. 'When do you go to the hospital again, young lady? Is it tomorrow?'

It was such a nonsensical question, it took her by surprise. He amplified it. 'I mean for your regular check-up and not for your work,' and he sounded rather irritated. 'I have some papers and mail to send to someone – a patient – in the private wing. It occurred to me that if you had the time tomorrow, you might deliver them in person and I should have the satisfaction of knowing they arrived safely. Also there might well be an answer.'

'I'll be glad to take them for you,' she said.

He gave her a locked brief-case. 'Deliver it, please, to Room C-5, and please remember to wait for an answer.'

Peter Lawrence collected Julie the next morning. Vera Leigh, who had been keenly interested in this new move on the part of the hospital, saw his car draw up outside and reported it.

'Well I never – it's that houseman, Peter Lawrence. Fancy having the medical staff taking you to the hospital, my dear. Are you sure he isn't sweet on you? There's something fishy about all this, what with getting on to the shop in person and arranging a job for you in the hospital and taking you out at night–'

'That wasn't Mr Lawrence,' Julie said. She had had to tell some of this to her landlady, to explain her absence every evening, but her explanation apparently didn't stop Gideon's wife from giving free play to her imagination. Julie hoped Mrs Leigh wasn't broadcasting all this to her women's meetings.

'Well, however it was, you're a lucky girl to have such attention bestowed on you. If it isn't a budding romance, then all I can say is, it's a pity they didn't think a bit more about Gideon and his condition. But there, it's always the pretty young girls without family responsibilities who get helped.'

Julie escaped to the waiting car. Peter Lawrence took his finger off the horn button when he saw her come flying out and he called out in alarm: 'Hey, take it easy. Wait till we've had time on that leg, before you start rushing about.'

'I keep forgetting,' she said, scarlet to the ears, as she clambered in beside him.

Peter Lawrence's car was an open one and looked as if it had been built in his home garage of odd bits of scrap and wire, but it went, as he cheerfully told her.

'If I hadn't been a quack, I'd have been a mechanic. I love messing about with cars.'

'You're sure you didn't mind fetching me this morning?' she asked him anxiously. 'I did say I could go by bus but Mr Hollidge sort of insisted.'

'Oh, he does, you know. We're used to his–' He broke off and she had the odd feeling he was going to say 'lame ducks'. He looked confused and amended what he had been going to say, to 'His friends he makes among the patients. There was a rather gorgeous ballet has-been. We hoped till the last he'd be able to do something for her, but there were complications. Still, she's very jolly about it all, and he has done a lot for her.'

'Yes, he was telling me about some of the patients he's friendly with,' Julie said. 'He's terribly nice, isn't he?'

'Quite a decent chap, actually, but considering everything, I suppose it isn't surprising he makes friends of the patients. I mean, with his home background, one isn't surprised.'

Julie held her breath and waited. Peter Lawrence wasn't very discreet and she didn't want to ask outright what he had meant.

'Do you live near the hospital?' she asked instead.

'Yes, we've got a poky little hole we call a flat, my wife and I. Every time she remembers the size of the place, she asks me rather tartly why I didn't go in for garage repair work instead of being a sawbones. There's more money in mending cars, d'you see?' and he sat laughing uproariously at his wife's wit.

They reached the hospital soon after that, and Peter said cheerfully, 'By the way, it'll probably be an ambulance pick you up tomorrow – do you mind? And the day after, it'll be a police car.'

'What for?' Julie asked, alarmed.

'Not to worry. No one else is stopping by, but the patrolmen are both ex-patients, and they made the offer, not us.'

Her examination was rather painful that morning. Adam was there, and a consultant Julie had never seen before. He was a big, silent, taciturn man, with heavy hooded black eyes behind very heavy glasses, and he had a big black beard that reminded her of a pirate more than a famous surgeon. When they had finished with her, it hurt to walk.

Adam told her to go and sit in the canteen and have some tea.

Then she remembered the brief-case and where she had left it. 'Would it be possible to take it up to the patient? As there's an answer, I might wait in his room, do you suppose? Or take it down in shorthand. It might help.'

'Rest first, then I'll see what I can arrange,' Adam said. He didn't look too happy about something. Julie thought it was her leg, and it made her feel depressed. Before Adam had raised her hopes, Julie hadn't really believed anything could be done. Now it was different, and already she had started seeing herself swimming again, and playing tennis. That was what Adam, at his gayest, could do for one, she thought ruefully.

He sat looking at her with such a sad expression while she drank her tea that she asked him what was wrong.

'Oh, nothing. Nothing concerning my work here, that is,' he said, passing a hand over his forehead. 'Look at the time – I must go back. I think I'll be able to see you to-morrow night, Julie, but I couldn't get out of my engagement tonight. What will you do?'

'The same as I did last night, I expect – wash some smalls and watch the television with my landlady's husband. There was a nice programme – planning a garden. And she knew nothing about it because she had a committee meeting. We had a gorgeous time with cocoa and cheese sandwiches in front of TV.'

He gave her a fleeting smile, then got up to go. 'Take care of yourself, my dear. See you tomorrow, with a bit of luck.'

When she had rested, a nurse came down to find her and took her over to the private wing. 'Sister says you can stay with him a little while, if you like,' the nurse said kindly. 'It's one of his good days and he does get so bored. Don't stay if you find he's getting tired, though, will you?'

'What's he like?' Julie asked curiously.

'Oh, he's a dear old boy, under his crusty manner,' she said.

Julie had never been into the private wing before. It was all gleaming ivory paintwork and dark red edge-to-edge carpets, and bowls and pots of flowers.

The room she was shown into had a lot of extras, provided specially for the patient. She noticed a portable television set and a small radio; and on a side table there was a very good portable typewriter.

The nurse said, 'Now, my dear, we have an unexpected visitor for you today. Sister says she can stay a little while if you'd like,' and she helped the patient up in bed and put extra pillows behind him.

He was a rather elegant old man, with a nicely trimmed white beard and moustache, and he had a vaguely Continental air about him that made Julie expect him to speak with a foreign accent. She was surprised

91

when he held out his hand for the brief-case and said, 'Good morning, young woman. You're from my shop. I recognise that brief-case. Have you brought the key with you?'

'No. Mr Gooch just gave me the brief-case. Nothing else.'

'Fine, fine,' he said wrathfully. 'Isn't that just like that old fool Gooch. He shouldn't have asked you to come, anyway, with a bad leg. Oh, yes, I noticed you limping in. I don't miss much. All I've got left to do – watch people, use my eyes. What did you do? Break your ankle, racing about? Most young people do.'

'No, I got hurt in a car crash,' she said, frowning. Who on earth was he?

'Did you? So did I. Let's swap notes. I was being driven by that nephew of mine. Young idiot. Too much of a dandy. I always want people not to go out with him, though there are plenty of folk around who are only too anxious to tell me it wasn't his fault. Say I'm a back-seat driver, they do. That's all very fine, but I could see he couldn't get through that space in the traffic, and I told him so and when he wouldn't listen, I grabbed the wheel.'

Julie flinched. 'Someone did that to me and the car skidded. It finished upside down with me pinned under it.'

'Oh. Did it happen like that with you?' He looked doubtful. 'Oh. Perhaps I shouldn't have grabbed the wheel. But confound it, that young fool irritates me so. If it hadn't been my chauffeur's day off, it would never have happened.'

'And you've been in here ever since, because of your injuries?' she asked sympathetically.

He glanced guiltily at her from under his bushy eyebrows, and then he laughed, a rather shame-faced laugh. 'To be honest, no. It was at first. Broke my ankle and it took a long time to heal. Then they discovered other things were wrong – shouldn't wonder if they didn't give me something to make me ill! They're like the garage people, do one job and make a couple more, to keep 'em in business!' he roared.

'You mustn't say things like that about the hospital. It's not true!' Julie was shocked and looked it.

'Why shouldn't I say what I like? Do you know who I am? I'm Howe, the Jeweller!'

He said it as if he were announcing that he were the long-lost heir to a throne or something equally important. It might have been rather funny, if Julie hadn't been preoccupied by wondering how it was that she hadn't realised who he was before. But in her heart she had never really believed that such a person existed.

'I'm sorry. I didn't know. Perhaps I'd better go now.'

'Why? Have you got something better to do?' He calmed down suddenly. 'I wish you wouldn't go, m'dear. I like you. Stay and talk a while to an old fellow, will you? No one comes to see me for pleasure. They come to get the signatures on cheques to pay the wages – that's all they want me for. And to sanction the buying and selling of the more important pieces. The rest of it is done by that nephew of mine. What do you think of him, eh? Tell me that now!'

'But I don't think I know your nephew, Mr Howe, do I?'

'You must do, if you work in the shop. That's what that old fool Gooch said you did, on the telephone. New shop-hand, and he was good enough to add that you were a quiet little thing with a flair for handling the less important customers. What a man! One of these days there's going to be a person come in who doesn't look important, who'll be so rich they'll want to buy the best pieces, and he'll miss it.'

'Please don't get so excited, Mr Howe. I'm sorry I don't know your nephew.'

'You must do! Don't side-track me, girl. And another thing that worries me about old Gooch – he's so obsessed with what people look like, he'll roll out the red carpet for one of the biggest rogues breathing, and we'll be robbed of all we possess. Got to have a good judgement of character, in the jewellery trade,' he finished, chewing his moustache.

He turned on Julie suddenly. 'And if my nephew Neville hasn't had his eye on you, I'll be surprised. Confess it now!'

'Neville! You mean Neville Stannard? Oh, *no!*'

'Ah, so he has! I thought as much. Well, remember what I said, and don't let him take you driving. And don't take too much notice of him, either. He's like old Gooch – over-impressed by what people seem to be. He'll settle for a rich wife. No eye for quality.' He looked sharply at Julie. 'What's the matter, girl? You've been out with him already, haven't you?'

'Yes, but I didn't know he was your nephew or I wouldn't have gone out with him. So that's why Mr Gooch said it wasn't suitable for me to be friends with him. I'm sorry, truly I am, but I'd got it into my head that he was only the store detective.'

'Store detective! Oh, my eye, that's a good one!' He kept repeating it, and laughing so much that the tears rolled down his cheeks and he started to cough and then to choke.

The nurse rushed in just as the alarmed Julie was on her way to the door to call someone.

'Now calm down, Mr Howe, do,' the nurse said. 'I think you ought to go,' she turned to Julie. 'He seems rather upset.'

'Upset! Don't be so silly, girl! She's done me good! She's made me laugh. Come again, what's-your-name! What is it, by the way?' he finished irritably, his coughing fit over, but his face still wet.

'Julie Quinn.'

'Julie Quinn,' he repeated. 'That's a jolly little name. I like it. I like you, too. Come again, will you, and cheer an old fellow up. And get someone to send me the key to that damned brief-case. What's the good of it if I can't get it open? I'll have to break it open with something, I suppose. Another good brief-case gone west.'

Julie heard him still grumbling, as the nurse hustled her out.

'What's really wrong with him?' she asked the nurse. 'I'm sure it was a pack of tall stories he told me.'

'I expect it was,' the nurse said composedly, though her eyes were dancing with amusement. 'He caused his accident himself for interfering with his nephew when he was driving.'

Julie made a wry face. 'He admitted that to me under pressure,' she said.

'Apart from that,' the nurse said, smiling and shrugging, 'there is nothing more than gout. Nothing, that is, that rest and a stringent diet won't improve but, of course, he hates it. While we can keep him in here, he'll be fine, but once he gets home and at the port again,' and she shrugged once more.

Julie went back to Fleckbury in the ambulance without having seen Adam. He occupied her thoughts. She forgot about the astounding news of Neville Stannard until she reached the shop. There he was, standing by the big circular glass case, as if waiting for her.

Mr Gooch had since found the key and was inclined to be fretful that the brief-case had gone without it. He called Julie into the office to question her about her visit to the old man. She contented herself by saying she had sat by his side at the ward sister's request, and that Mr Howe had asked that somehow the key should be sent to him.

'I could take it tomorrow morning, if you like,' she suggested, and Mr Gooch, in a relieved voice thanked her and gave it to her, with the warning that the case contained valuables, and she must on no account lose the key.

Neville came into the office as Julie was leaving. He followed her out. 'Julie, what did old Gooch want you for?'

At any other time she would have suggested to him that it was no business of his, but now, with the knowledge of his relationship to the head of the firm, it was rather different.

So she said collectedly, 'Mr Gooch was asking about the message he gave me to take this morning, *sir.*'

His brows drew down into a quick frown at that. He didn't like it, but he also knew that she was aware now, of who he really was.

'Oh. So that's how it's going to be, is it?' he said sourly.

'It ought to have been like that all along,' she told him collectedly, 'but I honestly thought you were just an employee like myself. I would have appreciated it if you'd told me from the first that you were Mr Howe's nephew.'

CHAPTER SIX

That night Boyd unexpectedly knocked at the neat front door of No 16 Canary Lane.

Vera was out again. She was speaking on a subject dear to her heart; organising other people's leisure. It didn't matter to her that she was only the stop-gap for someone else who was down with flu; this, she told Gideon severely, was her big chance and nothing in the world was going to stop her taking it. She waited for him to say something against that, but as he agreed, as always, she had nothing else to do but go, swallowing her disappointment.

She had left cold meat pie in the larder for both Gideon and Julie, and a rather dry rice pudding, but they didn't mind. They had already exchanged a secret look, and as soon as Vera had gone, they both crept out to the garden seat, to sit and watch the fish in the small pond beneath the wire.

'I read once,' Gideon began, 'about a chap who had a pond, and one by one his fish vanished. Couldn't make it out, till he rigs up a kind of shelter, all natural-looking, of twigs and such, and out he creeps at dawn to sit in there and wait.'

'What was it? A cat?' Julie guessed.

Gideon shook his head. She made three more guesses then to his delight she gave up.

'A heron!' he said triumphantly. 'Came over, large as life, like a blooming great aeroplane with its wings spread out against the dawn sky and down it swooped, and Bob's-your-uncle, another fish gone! So he had to put a stop to that.'

'What did your friend do, then?'

'Why, he put wire netting over the pond. That's where I got the idea from!'

Julie told him how resourceful it was of him, and refrained from expressing doubts about the existence of a heron in the vicinity of Fleckbury, because he would have been so disappointed. He was just about to remark on more reminiscences, when Boyd knocked.

Gideon went round to the front.

Julie wasn't pleased, when the two men came back together and she saw who it was. For one wild moment she thought it might have been Adam, finding he could get off tonight after all, and she was shocked at the way her heart leapt and raced at the very thought. Boyd brought her down to earth.

'Julie, love, how comes it you never told your good landlord that you had a relative in existence? 'Pon my word, I don't believe this excellent fellow really believes me when I tell him I'm your own cousin!'

Boyd at his best, charming Gideon with his elegance and his all-embracing charm, his man-to-man manner, his tenderness towards Julie. Boyd knew how to do it, when he took the trouble.

Julie made the required introduction without enthusiasm.

'He isn't exactly a cousin, Mr Leigh. Just a cousin by marriage and to be honest, I didn't expect to see him in Fleckbury.'

'I'm right glad to hear you have got someone belonging to you, lass,' Gideon said sincerely, and though he didn't say so (it being doubtful if he could have found the right words) his eloquent looks suggested that his pleasure also embraced the fact that Julie had such a smart and educated sort of cousin. Gideon was a worshipper of education. Anyone who had what he called the gift of the gab, could dazzle him at the drop of a hat. Boyd had it all right.

He sat down to tell Gideon casually but brilliantly about his visit to the Middle East, and the fortnight he spent in New York. Both were fiction, to the best of Julie's knowledge, and how Boyd managed to work in those two subjects and make them sound as if they had come up in the course of conversation, she never knew, but poor Gideon was Boyd's slave. He was just sitting listening, wide-eyed, respectful.

Julie said shortly, 'I'll make some coffee.'

Neither of them took any notice, so she went in the house, fuming, wondering how she could get rid of Boyd; wondering, too, what would have been the outcome of his visit if she had gone out with Adam, or Neville Stannard.

'We haven't had our meat pie, lass,' Gideon complained when she took the coffee out on a tray.

'Boyd is going,' Julie said firmly. 'We'll have our supper when he's gone.'

Gideon was shocked. 'No, lass, ask your cousin to share our supper. There's plenty. 'Tisn't friendly to send him away with an empty stomach.'

Boyd winced. 'In point of fact,' he said delicately, 'we neither of us need food now. We shall get sausages on sticks at the party, and a great number of other tit-bits that are

101

very satisfying.'

'What party?' Julie asked furiously.

'The party I told you about, sweetie,' Boyd said, with wicked effrontery, since they both knew he had never mentioned it before. 'You don't need to change. You'll do as you are. It's just sitting around on cushions listening to discs, and all that, but there's someone I rather wanted you to meet. Chap called Wyndham Fox, actually. Nice chap.'

'Not the Mr Fox who has that smart antique shop in the town?' Gideon broke in, excitement in his voice. 'Chap with a very smart way of dressing and sideboards? And his car – there is a car for you!'

'That's the very fellow,' Boyd said lazily. 'Friend of yours, Mr Leigh?'

Gideon flushed with pleasure, but vigorously denied such a thought. 'No, not a friend, but I know *of* him, by way of doing the odd job for him in the shop. Generous with his pay, he was. Oh, a very nice class of gentleman.'

'You go to the party, Boyd,' Julie said. 'I want a quiet evening at home with Mr Leigh.'

'Tell her not to be silly, Mr Leigh,' Boyd said, very seriously and earnestly. 'She'll listen to you. Tell her no one will notice her limp, because everyone sits and talks or listens to music. Tell her she ought to go out more, get her out of herself. That's what they advised her to do at the hospital, anyway.'

It was a master stroke, that last bit. Anything the hospital advised, Gideon was all for it. 'You go, lass, and do as your cousin says. I couldn't say more myself. You'll make me real miserable if you don't go with him, and that's a fact. Go on, now!'

So Julie went and got ready, seething inside her, and wondering what Boyd was talking to Gideon about beneath her window – within sight but just not near enough for her to hear.

She got through her change and wash in record time, but when she and Boyd at last got away in the second-hand car he had got hold of, she said to him, 'Very clever. Very nice work, convincing that poor man that you were a real friend to me. You're no friend to anyone, and I'd just like to know what you're up to, Boyd? Where are we going, anyway?'

'Like I said, sweetie, to Wyndham Fox's party, and in case I can ever hope to make you believe me, it is just as I said. A party, to take you out of yourself.'

'No. I don't believe it. We may be going to this Fox man's place, and it may be a party, but it won't stop there. I know it. With you, it has to be a cover for something else. Well, I'm not going to be involved in anything else with you, Boyd, so you can just jolly-well drive me back to Canary Lane again. I mean it.'

103

'All right, but do let's look in on the party first. It can do no harm and I did promise. After all, it won't hurt you to meet some more people. These are nice people. You heard how the old fellow talked about them. He was positively about to curtsey at the very thought of the upper crust in whose arms you were about to be thrust.'

'You're making game of him and I don't like it. He's nice, and you're not to go there any more. He doesn't understand your sort, Boyd. He'd never believe me if I told him you were just having him on.'

'Then don't tell him any such thing, sweetie. Here we are. Now do trust old Boyd, and take that suspicious scowl off your face, there's a dear. When you smile and look trusting, you've no idea how pretty you look, but just at this moment – no, definitely not pretty.'

She felt like hitting him, but they had arrived at a smart block of flats, and other people were going in, and one or two joined Boyd and he introduced her. Already he had made his mark, she noticed. Boyd in action, and it usually meant trouble. What trouble was lurking behind this evening's party?

They stayed for three hours. Julie forgot the time because after all it turned out to be quite a pleasant evening, one that (as Boyd had promised) made no claims on her bad leg, and in fact made her forget it, until she got up to go.

Wyndham Fox was a pleasant, good-looking young man with just that air of arrogance towards people who did jobs for him that it was easy to see how Gideon had been impressed. To Julie he delicately implied that she was one of the prettiest girls in the room and that he envied Boyd. There was nothing about Wyndham Fox that Julie could pin down or decide she disliked.

Boyd was cautious enough to take her from the party before she had a chance to remind him that it was getting late. It had been, after all, a cheese and wine party, and the wine hadn't been all that potent. Julie reluctantly admitted that even if she hadn't enjoyed herself (a thing hardly possible in Boyd's company) at least it had been a change.

'Well?' he said to her in the car going back to Canary Lane. 'Am I forgiven for plucking you from the protecting arms of Pa Leigh tonight?'

'Oh, I wish you wouldn't talk so about people I happen to like!' she fumed.

'Am I?' Boyd insisted.

'Let's put it this way, Boyd. At the moment I have nothing to complain about, but don't press your luck too far. And remember, I don't want you knocking at No 16 again.'

Boyd was silent, considering her, and then he smiled, an easy confident smile that she

105

didn't care for.

'All right,' he said, 'then I must contact you at the shop, mustn't I?'

'Don't you understand?' she burst out, between her teeth. 'I don't want you to contact me. I only went out with you tonight because you made it so difficult, playing upon poor Mr Leigh like that. Listen to me, Boyd. I mean this – I want you to leave me alone.'

'All right, then,' he agreed, a little too readily. 'I will leave you alone. I just thought we could be rather matey now the old troubles are over and I am no longer short of cash. In a sense, it was to be an attempt on my part to make it up to you for being such a confounded nuisance to you in the past. But if you don't want that, well, it shall be as you want it, honey.'

He touched her cheek with his hand cupped, a gesture that was impersonal yet somehow intimate at the same time. She didn't see how he could make it so, and it irritated her beyond measure. That was Boyd all over. Tell him he was being too friendly with you and he could somehow make it look as if he was in the right and you were finding unnecessary fault, she told herself angrily.

'I do want just that, Boyd,' she said, and left him.

He didn't linger. She heard his car go off in the normal way. There was nothing to show that he had taken umbrage or that they had

had words. Nothing to disturb Gideon Leigh, who had had a disappointing evening all alone, when he had looked forward to spending it with Julie. So long as she was all right, it would help him to compensate for his loneliness.

'Well, lass,' he said, when she went to find him in the shed at the bottom of the garden. 'How did you get on?'

'It was just as he said. A nice relaxed sitdown sort of party, with a lot of new people who were just lazing about in the same way. It was a change.'

'You did like it?' he insisted.

'Yes, I liked it, but I would have preferred to stay here and have a quiet chat with you.'

'Now that won't do, lass. You've got to get out and about with young people, people your own kind,' he said firmly. 'That young fella was a very nice sort of gent. You ought to let him take you about and meet people, you know.'

Boyd had done his work well. Julie gave it up and smilingly agreed with Gideon.

At that point, Vera returned, so mercifully there was no further opportunity to discuss Boyd.

In the days that followed, Julie nervously kept on looking over her shoulder, expecting Boyd to be there, smiling at her, making his presence so innocent yet so fraught with underlying meaning. She couldn't believe that he hadn't some wild scheme lined up to make money; a scheme that looked just wild but which was definitely not on the right side of the law.

Yet he didn't appear.

She worked in the hospital appointments office in the mornings, slipping up to see old Mr Howe just before she went off duty. She was transported in some way or other, to and from Fleckbury, and she spent peaceful afternoons in the shop, unworried by Neville Stannard who seemed to be losing interest in her. In the evenings, when possible, she spent time with Adam.

Sometimes it was just an hour, spent walking in the park near the hospital. Sometimes it was only ten minutes over a coffee in the delicatessen behind the hospital – depending on his clinics or how extra busy he was in his consulting rooms. Sometimes it was a whole evening.

Such an evening they spent together once on Chagwell Lake, with a small boat he hired. It was incredibly beautiful, that evening; an evening of rose and gold, with a lingering sunset and soft balmy air.

'You'll never make a good sailor,' he told her, with that new soft tone in his voice. 'You're all tensed up and your thoughts are only half on the job. What particular ghost is haunting you at the moment, Julie?'

She was alarmed that she had given

herself away so easily. 'Oh, I don't know. I should feel happier if Boyd would go right away and never bother me again,' she admitted. 'Not that he has been bothering me lately, mind you, but I know he's near, probably keeping me in sight, and I'm afraid he'll pop up again and that it will mean trouble for me.'

'What sort of trouble, Julie?'

'I don't know. Some fantastic scheme in which he wants me to take (so he says) a small and harmless part, only from there it goes wrong, and he never tells me what's really going on and I don't know just how bad the trouble is.'

'Then bluntly refuse to do anything he asks you to, and if he won't take no for an answer, refer him to me,' Adam said firmly.

'You make everything sound so simple,' she said, looking up at him with shining eyes. 'You don't know how glad I am that you're friends with me. I value your friendship so much.'

'Don't look at me like that, child or–' he said, frowning and looking away from her.

'Or what, Adam?'

'Or I shall probably forget I want to remain just friends with you,' he said crisply.

'Perhaps I don't want it to be just friends, not for ever, that is,' she said, very softly.

He pretended not to hear, and threw her a rope. 'Catch! Butter-fingers, when am I going to teach you to watch the thing, keep it in your eye, catch it and hold on to it?'

'I'm sorry,' she said miserably. It bothered her that she had no aptitude for handling a small craft, because she knew it was a hobby dear to his heart. 'I do try, Adam, but when you say "child" to me like that, you make me feel so young and silly and you take away what bit of self-confidence I have.'

'Oh, good heavens, that is the last thing I want to do.' He made fast the boat and helped her out on to the landing-stage and he didn't let go of her arms but stood looking down at her, so worried, so distressed, that she wished she hadn't exaggerated like that. 'You know that's true, don't you, Julie?'

'Well, why do you do it?' she cried. 'You're not all that much older than I am, are you? How old are you?'

She could have bitten out her tongue for that, and she felt she would have deserved it if he had prevaricated, as people do with children, and said something like he was too old to take that sort of cheek from her.

But he didn't. He told her the truth, sombrely, as if it made him unhappy to admit it. 'I'm thirty-five, Julie, and I happen to know only too well that you are exactly twenty-two.'

'Well, what's thirteen years?' she exploded. 'Oh, I'm being a nuisance, aren't I? Embarrassing you? I don't mean to, Adam. Only,

I'm so afraid that I shall find you like someone else better, like Neville Stannard, and then I shall see you going off with her, only you see, in the case of Neville, I didn't care particularly for him. I just felt horribly angry, to think he'd treated me like that. If it were you doing that to me, I don't think I could bear it. Adam, you would tell me if there was anyone else, wouldn't you?'

'My dear child, I wish you wouldn't talk like this!'

'But is there. Tell me now, at this minute, if you care for someone and I'm just being a nuisance.'

'Julie,' he said, taking her chin in his hand, 'there isn't a soul in the world I care for more than you.'

'Oh. I'm so glad!' The brilliance of that sudden smile of hers, cut him to the heart.

'I'm getting to like you too much,' he said shortly. 'It's got to stop.'

'But why, why?'

He watched the smile fade quickly, leaving her eyes hurt, misty. He felt so terrible for having done this to her that he was hard put to it not to gather her into his arms in that moment and tell her he loved her, pour out all the tumbled emotions that had been building up around her since she had first stepped into his cubicle in Out-Patients one morning. With an effort he braved himself, to say,

'Because we're going to be sensible and stay friends. We agreed on that at first and we're going to stick to that. It will be best for you, Julie, my dear. Believe me.'

He brushed her forehead with his lips, so briefly that the little action was over before she realised it, and he gave her a little push as he turned her round. 'Let's go. Quick forward march. The sun's going down and there's a chilly breeze springing up.'

The sun's going down. It certainly was, she thought, plunged into the depths of misery because she knew instinctively that he had been going to kiss her, and something had held him back. The discrepancy of years between them? If that were the case, then nothing could ever happen to alter it.

He drove her home in silence. Ordinarily it would have been a nice companionable silence, with no particular need for words. It had come to that lately.

But tonight it was a different sort of silence. Unhappy, a puzzling silence from her point of view; and from his, it was a silence in which he toiled around his troubled thoughts, blaming himself for not having handled the situation better. He should have been able to keep it from getting to that position; he should have been able to keep them just friends, as he had wanted from the start. But was that fair from her point of view? But then, who would have thought, he asked himself in exasperation, that she would have started to get a crush on him like that? Julie had seemed too sensible. He had only intended to be someone whom she could turn to for companionship, advice, a big brother.

Was that really true, his thoughts turned round to taunt him? Was that all he had wanted, really? Or had he not fallen in love with her from the first, and made excuses to himself, found ways to see her and twisted the motive so that it should seem all innocent like this? Face it, he told himself, you love her, and you'll be no good to her. Let her go.

Julie would have been astonished if she could have known the pattern his thoughts made. All she could think of was that she was so naïve that she was boring him now, though perhaps she hadn't at first. His flash of early interest was wearing thin. Much better to break the whole thing off, now, before his boredom showed much more plainly.

She tried to make herself say so, when he stopped the car outside the house of the Leighs. In that quiet little street, drenched with the scent of the flowers in the little front gardens, and the overtones of dank moist earth now the sun had gone down, she stood and stared miserably and tongue-tied, while Adam got out of his side of the car and walked round to open the gate for her, and to stand while she either found her key to open the front door, or walked round to the back. Tonight he took her shoulders in his hands, and stared at her so intently that again she thought he was going to kiss her.

'Good night, my dear. Take care of yourself,' he said at last, and abruptly let her go. For the first time he forgot to wait until she had let herself into the house.

She stood uncertainly at the gate, watching his car out of sight, feeling lonesome and rather choky.

As she went round to the kitchen door, tears pricked the back of her eyes. She wouldn't see him again socially, she told herself. He would see to that. That farewell of his had a sort of final ring about it.

She decided to just call out to the Leighs to let them know she was home safely, and to go straight up to her room.

She saw them sitting on the bench by the pond. The sight of two figures on that bench was so astonishing, that Julie halted. Vera sitting beside Gideon? She went down towards them to get a closer look at this phenomenon, but as she neared them, she saw that it wasn't Vera half hidden by Gideon's bulk. It was Boyd.

He made a lazy salute at her. 'I didn't come in, truly, love,' he protested. 'I just came to take a look at this chap's delightful garden, and he was out there and invited me in. Honour bright, that's truth, isn't it, Gideon?'

Gideon. So it was Christian names now.

'That's right, Mr Boyd,' Gideon answered. That was as near as he could get to taking the liberty of using Boyd's Christian name so far, but it would come. In time. Sooner than later. Boyd would see to that.

CHAPTER SEVEN

Like a cold wind worrying at a hole in a tooth, Boyd stayed long enough to fill Julie with anxiety, and then he gracefully took his leave.

The Leighs could find no fault with him. Gideon had found him looking with admiration at the blooms, as many another passer-by had done in the past, and he had succumbed to Boyd's open flattery, and naturally invited him in. Boyd stayed an hour – half an hour of that was spent with Julie. He left in time for Julie to still have anxious moments about him before she went to bed.

'He's a nice lad,' Vera remarked, as she cut bread and butter and made tea. 'Never overstays his welcome. Now that's what I like about a young chap. Are you going to wed him, my dear? Well, I know he's your cousin, but only by marriage, I think you said, and what's that to be a stumbling-block, I should like to know!'

'No, I'm not going to marry Boyd,' Julie said, rather shortly, and for once Gideon went so far as to frown at his wife and stop her further comments.

Julie didn't see Adam at the hospital the next morning. This wasn't surprising. It might well be that he was operating. There had been an intake of several emergencies the night before, from a factory accident. Yet she felt, when she went upstairs to the small private ward where Mr Howe was, that she had had a great loss.

Mr Howe noticed it at once.

'What's wrong with you, m'dear?' he roared at her. 'Bless me, I look to you to bring a ray of sunshine in – not make me feel I want to weep. Sit ye down by me and tell me all about it.'

She sat down, but she couldn't speak.

'Is it my nephew then?' By now, Julie had told him about how Neville had taken her out once or twice and then by-passed her for Dian Ackery.

She shook her head. 'No, I hardly ever see your nephew nowadays.'

It was easy to talk to him. Perhaps because he was in hospital, away from it all; perhaps because he was in such a tight little world of his own and lived on other people's eventful lives, Julie had told him bits of her own life in the time she had known Cedric Howe. He had been inclined to be amused about her early friendship with his nephew, but any reference to Boyd left him tight-lipped.

He wasn't pleased to hear the way Boyd was forcing himself back into her life.

'Bless me, girl, you're not fit to manage your own affairs! Send him packing, can't you? He's no good to you! You'd be far better off with my good-for-nothing nephew than this – this Boyd What's-his-name!'

'I'm not going to marry Boyd!' Julie said, in an alarmed voice. It wasn't the first time that such a suggestion had been made. The Leighs had already made it.

'He'll get you,' Cedric growled.

'Oh, no, I don't want to marry him – I don't want to marry anyone except–' and she broke off before his pitiless stare and wondered what was happening to her, that she should let her guard down in this way. Almost blurting out how she felt about Adam!

'Oh, got your sights on someone else, eh,' Cedric Howe commented. 'You're a sensible girl. Why don't you get yourself fixed up, if you care for the fellow? Don't hang around single – a pretty girl is fair game for the scamps. Always was – nowadays worse than ever. If I had a pretty granddaughter, I'd get her married off in no time. Only safe way, you know. Take an old fellow's advice.'

'What would he give by way of advice, if he knew that the man only wanted to be friends and not to be in love?' Julie said ruefully.

'Oh, is that the lay of the land? Sounds as if he's married already,' the old man grunted. 'Don't like the sound of that at all. Can't be trusted to look after yourself, can you, m'dear?'

Julie whitened, slowly, so that the whole of her being seemed to be freezing. Her hands began to shake, and she couldn't even see straight, for thinking of the terrible thing Cedric Howe had just suggested. Adam – married already?

She shook her head to clear her vision. 'No, he can't be,' she muttered. 'He wouldn't do that to me. Besides, I asked him, I begged him, to tell me if there was anyone else, and he said there wasn't. He said that there was no one in the world he cared for more than me. Or words to that effect.'

'Then if that's the case and he still only wants to be friends, then you'll permit an old fellow to remark that the chap sounds a perfect bounder!' Cedric said wrathfully.

'No, not him,' Julie whispered. 'Not him. You don't know him. You don't know what he's like.'

And yet, even as she said it, she realised that in all probability, Cedric did know Adam – knew him well!

'What does he do for a living, if one may ask?' Cedric said tartly.

Now she would have to tell him who it was, Julie told herself, furiously. What had made her go so far as this? Amusing a patient was one thing, but revealing her inmost secrets was another!

The door opened after the briefest tap, and a young woman backed in with a trolley.

'Oh, if it isn't our little book lady,' Cedric said, in a kind voice he might have used to a child.

Julie studied the young woman who had produced this change of manner in him. She clumsily got the trolley through the doorway and allowed the door to slam, then she turned to the man in the bed with her own hand over her mouth in mock dismay.

'Sorry, chum,' she said, in a slurred but educated voice. 'Aren't I the end? Oh, lor, didn't know you had a visitor. Now I'll have to get the old barrow out again. Why didn't you put an Engaged on the door,' she howled at Julie.

'Take it easy, m'dear,' Cedric cautioned her. 'Bring your trolley over and let's have a look at the books you've got. This is just a little friend of mine who also works in the hospital. Julie Quinn, from the Appointments Office.

She's also part-time in my own shop, so you see, I've got a proprietory interest in her, too.'

'Why, has she been at the same tricks as I used to?' the young woman asked with sudden interest.

'No, no, nothing like that,' Cedric said, alarmed for the moment. Then he laughed. 'I mean I had an interest in her because of her being one of my own employees.'

'Oh. Does she know about me?' the young woman asked.

'No, but I propose to tell her now that you used to be an actress, a very good one,' Cedric said smoothly. 'Julie, this is Rosalind Osborne.'

Julie fancied the young woman looked very much relieved though she herself couldn't quite see why. They gravely acknowledged each other, then the conversation swerved to the books. Cedric made a lot of it and took two or three, although Julie had the impression that he hadn't really wanted them.

Julie got up and limped to the door, holding it open for the trolley of books to be pushed through without disaster. Rosalind stopped to stare at Julie's leg.

'What happened to you?' she asked, in her queer, low, slurred voice. Julie thought she might have been doped; it was like she herself had been after she had taken too many cold cure tablets once.

'I was pinned under a car,' she said, quietly.

Rosalind shuddered. 'Bully for you, chum,' she drawled, and hastily fled. They heard her trolley rattling along the polished corridor and her perilous heels click-clicking.

Then Julie shut the door, with a rueful smile. 'What a strange person. Was she really an actress?'

Cedric nodded. 'Not a world-shaker, mind you, but quite a competent lass on the stage. There's a tragic case for you.'

'Tragic? How tragic?' Julie wanted to know. She had to go soon, so she just stood behind her chair, holding its back rail, while she exchanged the last few words with him before going.

'Why, d'you see, those tricks she refers to – she got too fond of the drink. She's been away in a Home, actually. Sent her out as cured, but I wonder!'

'Oh, how awful!'

'Yes. Yes, it was rather awful, Julie, when you think that if she hadn't married a doctor and had to leave the stage to please him, she might have been happy, hard-working, and not in that state at all.'

'A doctor? Oh! Which one is she married to?' Julie asked, and for no reason at all, she felt frightened.

Cedric didn't seem to hear her. Sometimes he didn't directly answer her, but went on talking, pursuing a thought of his own. 'Yet one can't blame the husband. Comes of a well-known medical family. Probably be a big-shot himself in the near future. Wouldn't want his wife careering all over the country in rep. That was all she was, of course – little rep actress. No, it wouldn't have done, really. A man needs his wife by him. Still, tragic, yes. Tragic, very!'

The sister came in then. 'Oh, you still have your visitor, Mr Howe. I wondered if you were alone. Well, now, we're going to pull you about. Mr Jancy is here, with Mr Hollidge, and they think it might be a good time to have another look at those ribs.'

Julie didn't want to run into Adam just now, so she hastily said a brief good-bye and slid out.

Adam was coming along the corridor with the other consultants. Although he didn't stop talking, or acknowledge Julie, his eyes met hers and held them, and she felt that thrill go through her that always accompanied the sight or sound of him these days. As if he were a dentist and had touched a nerve. No, not exactly – more like if you touched an electric light switch that wasn't safe. A tingling, not unpleasant, but a little frightening, rushing through one, right to the end of one's fingers and toes, and the top of the scalp.

She hurried on down to the Appointments

Office, and looked in at one of the glass windows where the patients put their cards through, and waited for their files.

'Have you heard how I'm to be taken back to Fleckbury today, Joan?' she asked the clerk who pushed the window up.

'Bert's ambulance, Julie,' the girl said cheerfully, and left the window open, to return to her desultory conversation with another clerk. This was almost at the end of the clinics. Only the odd out-patient was left waiting. They could afford to stand and lean against the counter for a minute or two.

The hall was filled with comings and goings, mostly people going off duty for lunch. The rep actress, Rosalind Osborne, slouched through, without her trolley. Her hair wasn't very tidy. Those complicated styles, Julie thought, really needed a lot of attention, if they weren't to look awful. She needed, too, to repair her make-up, but apparently she was in no mind to stop. She raised a hand in greeting to one of the porters, who grinned back at her.

'That awful creature!' the other clerk said wrathfully. 'How on earth did a nice man like that come to marry her?'

Julie stood there, stiff and still. Now she would hear whose wife that girl was.

But the speaker choked suddenly and when Julie looked round she was nursing her ankle. 'What did you do that for?' she complained.

The other clerk was looking at Julie in dismay. She had clearly meant the kick as a warning because Julie was standing there. The first girl coloured and moved away.

What was all that about, Julie wondered.

Bert came in, looking for her. 'Oh, there you are, miss! Look slippy – my lunch is calling me. Good hot roast, today, at home. Daren't keep the missus waiting.'

He stood smiling broadly at Julie as she limped over to him and they walked out to the ambulance.

Rosalind Osborne was hanging about. She turned to Bert as Julie climbed up.

'How about a lift, Bertie boy,' she drawled.

'No. No, none of that, now,' Bert said. 'The last time I gave you a lift, you made me put you down at the "Rose and Crown" and wasn't there a fine old shindy! No, I promised myself – no more lifts for you on my ambulance. No!'

He started up the engine and carefully backed out. 'You don't half have to keep your wits about you on this job,' he grumbled, to himself. 'My ears are still stinging from the things Mr Hollidge said to me, last time I copped it with that madam! Cor!'

Julie sat there, the frozen feeling coming back. It dawned on her all of a sudden, whose wife that girl was. So that was why the other clerks wouldn't talk about it in front of her!

She knew better than to ask Bert outright, so she tried it in reverse, just to check. How she kept her voice steady, she never knew, as she said casually, 'Is Mrs Hollidge really in danger of going back to drinking?'

'Is she heck!' Bert said feelingly. Then he was silent, thinking over the fact that Julie had mentioned her by name. 'Oh, you knew about that, did you, miss? I often wondered, seeing as you seemed to be a pet of his, if you'll pardon the liberty. Still, he do make pets of his patients, and so long as you know how the land lays, it's all right, I suppose. It's not for me to say, anyway, but a nice girl like you—'

'Yes, I get the message, Bert,' she said. 'If you drop me here, it will do, thank you,' and she pointed to the row of shops just round the corner from Canary Lane. If she stayed listening any longer to Bert talking about that subject, she would scream, she told herself.

He waved to her and drove back the way he had come, unaware that she couldn't see where she was going for the tears blinding her eyes, and that she couldn't hear the sound of the traffic or a nearby pneumatic drill, because of the chorus deafening her own ears: Adam's married, Adam's married.

Quite suddenly she knew that she couldn't go back to the house for lunch. She slipped into a callbox and telephoned the next door neighbour to call over the fence that she had been delayed and would have lunch out. Vera and Gideon would notice she was upset and have the truth out of her.

She went into a delicatessen and bought two ham rolls and went into the churchyard to sit and eat them, but they almost choked her. So that was why he only wanted to be friends. Why couldn't he tell her he was married, and so prevent her from letting him see that she cared. Why couldn't he have saved her that?

Why, she asked herself in despair, did men treat her so badly? Boyd taking her for granted and using her in his shabby little schemes. Neville using her for fun while he was secretly playing up to a rich customer. And now Adam...

She knew she would never be able to go and see Cedric Howe again, either, for fear he got the truth out of her. She wished she had never gone to that beastly hospital.

It was in a decidedly upset frame of mind that she went to the shop that afternoon, and during the slackest time, Boyd walked in.

Julie thought she was going to faint at the sight of him. He looked so dapper, so well-tailored, so right, somehow, for the sort of shopping he had obviously come in to do. He strolled purposefully past Julie, ignoring her, and made for the counter where the expensive cuff-links were. Wyndham Fox, equally elegant and casual, was behind him.

Julie watched them in amazement. They would, of course, only make a pretence of buying. They would look at everything of value in the shop, and go out, having spent nothing. At least, those were Boyd's tactics. Now it remained to be seen whether Wyndham was in that sort of game with him, or genuine.

Julie couldn't stop herself from staring at them. She was prevented from giving herself away, by the arrival of a customer at her own counter, and the appearance of Neville Stannard.

Her heart began hammering. Would he recognise Boyd as the man he had spoken of, with dark glasses, loitering outside the shop that day? The man who had asked if Julie Quinn worked there, the man to whom Neville had said curtly that he didn't know anything about it?

Boyd's own manner assured Julie that such would not be the case. As the time went by, Julie noticed that Mr Gooch was doing his special 'red carpet' act, the failing Mr Howe had noticed in him. Mr Howe hadn't realised what true words he had been speaking when he had said that one day a rogue would walk into the shop and fool Mr Gooch into thinking he was dealing with a wealthy and important customer. It was happening now.

Mr Gooch was fawning on them. Neville Stannard was called over. A purchase was made. Wyndham Fox was writing a cheque.

Charlie Carr, the assistant that Julie didn't like, strolled over to her. 'Money is being splashed about,' he murmured, out of the side of his mouth. 'Names are being bandied. The chap with the cheque-book knows the duchess.'

'The duchess?' Julie murmured, bewildered.

'The one who is nibbling at the Collar,' he explained patiently. 'You know – the one I told you about.'

Something awful was going to happen before their eyes. Julie didn't know what, but she had felt like this before, when Boyd had been trying to pull off one of his schemes. The one that had fallen through and Boyd had gone away for a long time...

Should she call the police? But what could she say they were doing? Buying some expensive cuff-links with a cheque that, for all she knew, might be a good one. After all, Wyndham Fox had an antique shop in the town. He was well-known locally. He had an expensive flat and knew people with money. So ... what was wrong in what they were doing? Yet she knew in her heart that something was wrong somewhere.

They were looking at the Mendellini

Collar. They were all standing round it. Little snatches of memory teased Julie. Boyd in mischievous mood, talking about how he would rob a museum. Things like pushing a piece of wax into the key hole and getting an impression to make a new key, all the while he would be talking fast and no one would notice. But he couldn't do that here, Julie's thoughts clamoured, because the Collar was taken out at night and put in the safe. He couldn't replace the Collar with a fake while he was looking at it because he would need to have the collar to make the copy, so *that* wasn't possible. Besides, Boyd was only an amateur, not a top-level jewel thief. But a daring amateur...

She was so glad when they went. Mr Gooch and Neville Stannard walked them to the door. Mr Gooch called them a taxi. Trust Boyd not to drive up in his second-hand car. But where was Wyndham's over-smart racing car?

She felt sick and wished it was time to go home. Neville Stannard strolled over to her counter.

'What's the matter, Julie? You look terrible,' he said.

'It's so hot,' she said faintly.

'Well, it's tea-time. Go out and get some tea for a change,' he said. 'Go on. Get your-self ready. I'll go with you. I want to talk to you.'

'No. Please, no, I don't really want to,' she protested. Anything, rather than that.

But Neville, as always, insisted.

The tea-shop was rather dark, but cool. Quiet, overlooking a small paved yard with a tree in the middle, and in one corner a thin trickle of water from a cherub's mouth made a musical tinkle.

'Rather nice, isn't it?' Neville murmured, watching her face. 'Care to sit out there? It's warm enough.'

'No. No, thanks. I mustn't stay long. Mr Gooch doesn't like it as it is, me not being in the shop in the morning. I'm sure he's suspicious of this job I have at the hospital.'

'Yes, and not only the job,' Neville agreed. 'I hear you visit my uncle pretty regularly.'

'Visit? Hardly that. Just a few minutes to exchange a word or two with him, and that wasn't my idea.'

'Oh. Whose was it?'

'Mr Gooch's, in the first place, to take over a brief-case. But he forgot the key, so I had to take it the next day. Then Mr Howe asked me to drop in when he heard that I worked in the hospital.'

'Why?'

'I don't know. A new face, I suppose. He told the nurse in my hearing that I was good for him because I made him laugh.'

'Does he know you work for us?'

'Oh, yes,' she said collectedly, and although

she didn't add the 'sir', it sounded as if she might have been going to. 'He knows I'm just a counter-hand.'

That was a childish trick, she reproved herself, because she knew it would make him wince. Funny, how touchy they were about such things.

'Does he ever mention me?' Neville persisted.

'Once, the first time I met him. He seemed surprised that I didn't know you were his nephew. Very amused when I told him I thought you were the store detective.'

'He would be,' Neville said grimly. 'What else did he say?'

Julie decided not to mention that the old man had hinted that the accident had been Neville's fault, as Cedric Howe had retracted afterwards, so after a minute, she said, 'He hasn't mentioned you since that day. We talk of other things.'

'When you ladle out reproof, Julie, it has the back-kick of a mule,' Neville drawled. 'All right, you find more interesting things to discuss. I believe I made a mistake in not keeping up my friendship with you. Why did I let you get away with it, ditching me for some chap at the hospital?'

'It was you who did the ditching, I believe,' she reminded him, but a smile curved her mouth at his annoyance. The smile touched her lips only. She didn't feel like smiling really. His reference to Adam reminded her again that Adam had done his share of treating her shabbily. So he was married, was he? Anger welled in her. Well, she wouldn't sit around waiting for some other man to come along and take her out; why not accept a date from Neville? There was nothing in it, but if Adam Hollidge were tempted to casually call for her again, then he could jolly well find she was out with someone else.

'Am I never to be forgiven for that one lapse, when I got caught up with a rich customer?' Neville asked whimsically.

'I didn't say so,' Julie murmured, playing with her pastry fork.

'You mean you'll come out with me again? Why, you little devil, I believe you're having me on a bit of string.'

'I didn't say I wouldn't come out with you again, did I? Where were you thinking of taking me?'

'Well!' he exploded, and then he laughed. 'I'll strike while the iron is hot. Dinner, I think, and then a show. I can get some tickets in a hurry, I have no doubt. And Julie, while we're on the subject, whatever my uncle may have said about Dian Ackery and me–'

'I'm not interested in how you feel about any of the customers,' Julie put in coldly. 'We're just talking about the odd date.'

He refused to be affronted. He had had his way over another date with her. He hadn't been stood up indefinitely by any girl: that was the most important point with him. If he wanted to break it off with Julie, that was his affair, but he couldn't countenance Julie holding him at a distance.

When they reached the shop, it was empty. It was the quiet time of the afternoon. Yet Mr Gooch was in a very ruffled state. He asked Neville Stannard to go into the office with him.

Charlie Carr drifted over to Julie. 'Our friend Mr High-and-Mighty Gooch has been taken for a ride, I think,' he said, looking very pleased.

'What does that mean?' Julie asked him, apprehension beginning to creep back again.

'Remember those two chaps who were in earlier, and who were given the V.I.P. treatment?'

She nodded. Boyd and his friend. Her heart began to quicken its beats unpleasantly. Now she would know what was behind it all.

'Well, the fact is, one of them came back and said he'd dropped a valuable tie-pin while he was in the shop. In a bit of a state about it, he was.'

'Which one was it?' Julie breathed.

'Not the one who did the buying – Fox, his name was – but the other one.'

Boyd. Yes, this was the way he played his hand.

'Did they find it?' Julie asked.

'Yes, at last, under the Holy of Holies.' That was Charlie's satirical way of referring to the round glass case on its stand, containing the Mendellini Collar. The stand was solid-based, almost but not quite, to the carpeted floor. Just room to put the hand under and get out something that had been dropped and rolled or kicked under.

'And guess what else he found while he was in the shop?' Charlie crowed.

Julie was white now. 'What?' she asked.

'The Ackery girl. I nearly laughed out loud, it was so smooth. His pal had turned up by then, and dear Dian Ackery drifted in, and poor old Gooch didn't know who to give the V.I.P. treatment to first, and old Stannard not there to do the honours to his girl-friend.'

Neville came out of the office at that moment, Gooch behind him. Neville looked grim.

'I'll be back,' Charlie Carr said, and slid away, after his usual fashion. By the time Neville came down to Julie's counter, Charlie had found a customer and was earnestly showing her a canteen of cutlery which she didn't want.

'Is anything wrong?' Julie forced herself to ask Neville as he went by.

'What? Oh, no, not really.' But he looked far from pleased.

A little later, he did come back to Julie to tell her very briefly, that he had managed some tickets for a show and that it would be all right for that evening.

Later still, Charlie Carr drifted over again, unholy joy on his thin unlikeable face. 'Stannard's had his girl whipped from him,' he said. 'That chap with young Fox, this afternoon, picked her up, cool as you please.'

'Picked her up?'

'I say, you always repeat what a fellow says. Can't you think up something original to say?'

Julie had never felt such deep despair. Of course she could think up something original to say – plenty. But it would be lunacy to put her present thoughts into words.

'If you want it in words of one syllable,' Charlie Carr said impatiently, 'the Fox chap said he knew her and in no time at all they were all chatting away, ignoring poor old Gooch, and Fox's friend suddenly says a curt good afternoon over his shoulder, and takes the Ackery wench by the arm and whoops! she's away out of the shop with him, looking pretty pleased with herself. Of course, it might just be that she wanted to wipe our pal Stannard's eye, but it was queer in a way.'

'What was queer?' Julie asked him, flattering him by hanging on his words, not because Carr interested her but because this was also Boyd's brilliant technique. A side

135

act that would annoy people and take their minds off what he was really doing.

'Well, the way that chap did that pick-up. It was a pick-up, I think, because I wasn't feeling so sure of that Fox chap's insistence that he was a friend of Dian Ackery. Probably knew her as a customer. But that other fellow – it was smooth, just *smooth*.'

CHAPTER EIGHT

The following afternoon when Julie left work, she found Boyd waiting for her at the bus-stop.

'The old jalopy is just round the corner,' he murmured, taking her arm. 'And I don't want any excuses about coming with me, either.'

Puzzled, she went with him. She was tired. It had been one of 'those' days – difficult at the hospital, and difficult in the shop, and she had had to cut her lunch-hour short, too. There was still a flap on, and she hadn't heard all there was to hear about it.

All in all, she was glad enough of the lift, even though it was Boyd giving it. She got in beside him without a word, and he didn't speak until he had nosed his car painfully out of the dead end where he had parked it, into the stream of home-going traffic. Later tonight this main road would be very quiet, deadly; at the moment it was almost as mad a clutter of traffic and people as the busiest parts of Eltonstock.

'Where were you last night?' Boyd asked, as soon as they were out of the main press of cars and buses. 'I called for you but the house was empty.'

'Mrs Leigh was at a meeting, I suppose. I don't know what Mr Leigh was doing.'

'But we haven't heard yet where you were,' Boyd said. He wasn't pleased.

'If you want to know, I went out with a friend to dinner and a show.'

'Which friend?'

'Boyd, are you out of your mind? I don't have to account to you who my friends are!' she flushed.

'All right, if you don't want to tell me, I'm sure it can't matter,' he said, after a pause. He was calming down now. He added, 'As it happened, I wanted you rather urgently.'

'Then you should have contacted me much earlier, shouldn't you?' she said, tiredly. 'Here we are.'

'You sound very relieved, but it so happens that I have a few things to say before you go into that house,' Boyd said rather grimly. 'I thought you were going steady with some type at the hospital?'

'Well?' Julie asked, very quietly indeed.

Boyd considered her. They had had their clashes in the past. He could push her so far, but there was always a point where he had to pull up sharply and alter his tactics, if he wanted to keep her allegiance. 'Now I hear that you are great friends of old Howe himself.'

'What about it?' Julie flashed.

Boyd settled back in the car and the cat-got-the-cream look came into his face. 'But that's marvellous, if it's really true, love, but why didn't you tell me? It would have made it all a lot easier.'

'How would it?'

'Not to worry,' he said, and leaned forward to open the car door for her. 'Out you get. I shan't be coming in tonight.'

'Oh, no, Boyd, this won't do,' Julie said angrily. 'You've questioned me pretty thoroughly. Now you answer a few questions. What was all that about yesterday, in the shop? How did you persuade Wyndham Fox to go into something with you?'

Boyd pleased to look astonished. 'Sweetie, what *are* you talking about? The old lad genuinely wanted to buy something, bless his little bank balance, and he took me along to help him choose. Cuff-links are not his strong line and he took every tiny word of advice I dropped into his willing ear. How could you be so uncharitable and suspicious?'

'And who were you helping when you walked off with Dian Ackery? Didn't anyone tell you she is Neville Stannard's girl-friend?'

Boyd's eyes widened. 'Now how was I supposed to know that, seeing as I have it on very good authority that you and he were having a little heart-to-heart in a certain rather exclusive tea-shop yesterday afternoon and that you've been out with him several times before?'

'That's none of your business, Boyd!'

'Oh, but it is, sweetie. I have to know who is which, now don't I? But not to worry. I won't go out with her again. She's a very boring girl indeed. She thinks that money's everything, a thing I have never ascribed to.'

'Oh, Boyd, really I can't talk to you, you give such stupid answers,' Julie exploded. 'Neville is furious–'

'Is he, though?' and Boyd looked pleased.

'–and there's an awful flap on in the shop. Did you really drop an expensive tie-pin?'

'I did indeed. And don't insult me by saying you didn't know I had one. It was a gift from a grateful – er – partner, shall we say? One that you don't know. Anyway, how can they be cross with me for going back for it? I found it all by myself.'

'Did you?' She was at once interested. 'How?'

'By using my sense and remembering

where I could have dropped it. It must have been while we were looking at that hideous Collar in the glass case. I got entangled with someone or something–' and he was grinning widely now.

Her heart started hammering again. 'Boyd, they – there's a rumour – well, I heard someone in the shop say something about the little bracelet that matches the Collar–'

'Equally hideous piece,' he pronounced.

'No, not the one with all the coloured stones, but the slender diamond bracelet. It's not genuine, yet I don't see how the real one could have got out of the glass case and a fake put in.'

He touched her cheek. 'Don't be so distressed, sweetie. Even old Boyd isn't clever enough to have replaced that piece – or any other in that case – not that I would have wanted to, mind you. Too distinctive to be got rid of.'

'Then why are they so jumpy about the pieces getting stolen? And what has happened to the original piece?' she fretted.

'It's my guess that a set of fakes have been made (well, copies, if the word "fake" upsets you) and that old fool Gooch has got them mixed. Don't worry, it'll turn up again, somewhere, someday. Now I must go.'

'But Boyd–' she began.

'No buts, my sweet. Believe me, old Boyd is not the guilty party. Mind you,' he said, a wicked grin lighting his eyes, 'having had an original replaced by a copy, the lordly firm of Howe the Jeweller wouldn't expect it to happen again, would they?'

'What are you thinking, Boyd?' He always alarmed Julie when he started talking in this way.

'Just thinking, my sweet, just thinking.'

'About what? Tell me! If you're thinking that whoever did it could get away with it again—'

'No, sweetie, I think old Gooch has blundered. But if someone else wanted to try it, he'd look jolly silly, wouldn't he? Funny, the thought coming up like this. You see, there is someone who— Oh, forget it.'

'No, Boyd! You're to finish what you were going to say,' Julie stormed.

'All right, since you wish it. I happen to know of a lady who has a title, an invitation to a ball about to be given by a visiting foreign royalty, and no necklace to wear, but the lady has just enough money stashed away to pay a nice little fee for the loan (the loan only, mark you) of the Mendellini Collar for the occasion.'

'Are you mad? How could anyone borrow it and get away with it? And anyway, how could anyone wear it without it getting around?'

'As I said, forget it, sweet.'

'But what makes you think it's even worth

thinking about?' she asked, fear goading her to at least put the questions to him. 'I mean, you'd have to know someone inside–'

He nodded, looking pleased at her brightness.

'Not me, Boyd, not me!'

'No, sweetie, not you, although it's only information anyone would want for such a job, and goodness knows, you've passed on enough of that already. I guarantee I could draw a plan of the place, with all the switches of the alarms, and I know of the perfect way in.'

'How?'

'From you, my sweet.'

'But I haven't told you a thing, Boyd, and I wouldn't, either! You know that!'

'I do indeed, sweetie. You wouldn't tell old Boyd a thing. No cousinly love whatever. Don't I know it? Forget the whole thing, sweetie. Off you go now. Enjoy yourself,' and he almost pushed her out of the car.

'Go and ask your pal Gideon how I would know the inside story,' he called out, as he put the car into gear and roared it up the street with a tantalising wave of his hand.

Gideon Leigh. Oh, heavens, had Boyd got it out of him? One evening Julie had amused him, telling him of the elaborate precautions taken in the jewellers. She had trusted Gideon, trusted him because of his inarticulate ways and his retiring nature. Gideon would be the last person to tell anyone else, because he couldn't talk about the things he wanted to, let alone betraying anyone else's secrets. But with Boyd skilfully probing, saying the wrong to get the right, what effect would that have?

Julie couldn't believe it.

She went wearily across the road and into the house. Vera was, as usual, talking. Talking about the state of the larder, the need for new hooks and hinges; talking about the way nothing got done if she didn't chivvy people around to stir their stumps, as she put it; and talking slyly but purposefully about those people who would kill themselves to get things done in the garden, but nowhere else in the house.

Julie met Gideon's eyes as he glanced up from his plate briefly. She wanted to signal to him that she had something to discuss with him but this was not the time or the place.

Vera suddenly turned round on Julie. 'And why aren't you getting ready to go out with that nice young cousin of yours, my dear? Don't you let Gideon keep you talking!'

Gideon looked affronted for a moment, then gave up and went out of the room.

'It isn't Boyd tonight, but perhaps I'd better not waste any time,' Julie said pacifically.

As soon as she could decently break away from the meal-table, she went to find Gideon

143

but he wasn't in the shed or anywhere in the garden.

The man next door straightened up and peeped at her over the fence, casting a wary eye to see if Vera were anywhere within ear-shot.

'He's gone to the river, miss,' he offered. 'He said to tell you he'd like a word with you, if you wasn't in a rush to get out.'

'I want to speak to Mr Leigh myself,' Julie said. 'Whereabouts near the river will I find him?'

'Know the old boat-house? He'll be round the back. There's a few stone steps. Like as not he'll be sitting on them. Don't let his missus know, though. She worries,' he said, pulling a face to show that he, too, was in the habit of using this bit of fiction.

Julie took a raincoat and limped off down the road. The sky looked dark and thundery. She wondered what had possessed Gideon to go out on an evening like this. He used to stay near the choice blooms and endeavour to cover them against the force of the rain when a storm threatened.

He was where his neighbour said he would be. He had put on his shabby oilskin and an ancient turned down tweed hat. He sat hunched on the steps, staring at the water.

'Hello, it's me,' Julie said. 'Your neighbour told me where you'd be.'

'Hello, lass. Did my wife say anything

about me slipping out?'

'No, as a matter of fact, I believe she thinks you're in the potting shed. She thinks I've gone out with a friend. She thought it might be Boyd but I had to tell her it wasn't.'

He nodded. 'She do worry a mort, and that's a fact.'

'Yes,' Julie said. 'About my cousin Boyd—'

'Ah, yes, about him,' Gideon agreed, and looked consideringly at her.

'He's only related by marriage. Not a blood relation,' she said, urgently.

'So you said, lass.'

'What I'm trying to say is, you've been deceived by him. He isn't nice, not really.'

She expected an indignant defence of Boyd, but there was none forthcoming. Gideon sat looking at her so long that she squatted on the top step beside him. 'He wins people over talking,' Julie went on.

Gideon nodded slowly, still not speaking.

'And he makes you think things are different to what they are.'

'What are you trying to tell me, lass?' Gideon asked.

'I don't know how to say it. You're so nice, and a good friend of mine, but you believe people are all as nice as you are, and I can't offer you proof that Boyd isn't. I can only tell you what I know of him.'

'Go on,' Gideon said.

She swallowed, and plunged into telling

Gideon the same story she had told Adam Hollidge. About the way Boyd had always behaved, about that special day when she had had to drive him, and had got pinned under the car; about the way he had tracked her down, and what the significance of that party at Wyndham Fox's flat had been.

Gideon just sat and watched her face, the play of emotions there, the movements of those sensitive hands of hers.

At last she got to the point of the story; what had happened that afternoon at the shop, and now today, and the things Boyd had said to her. Then she stopped and stared at Gideon.

'And you think, lass, that by his saying the wrong to get the right, he'd have got out of me what you told me about the shop.' It was a statement, not a question.

'I know you wouldn't mean to tell him anything I'd told you, in confidence,' Julie said miserably.

'Nor I wouldn't, in the ordinary way,' Gideon said, unhappily. 'You see, t'wasn't like that. No asking nor giving of information. What really happened was some talk about private detectives, and all I said was that it seemed Howe's had got one. "That's where you're wrong," says he. "They haven't." And he told me a lot more about Howe's that agreed with what you'd told me, so I thought he knew, and there was no

146

harm in agreeing with him. Especially him being someone belonging to you, lass.'

'I should have warned you of what he was like,' Julie fumed. 'I shouldn't have told you even the smallest thing about Howe's, so as not to burden you with the knowledge, only they seemed such innocent little details of interest to you, as you'd fixed burglar alarms in shops like that Wyndham Fox. I just never thought Boyd would come here and use the information.'

'Any use asking you what he'd want it for, lass, if he isn't the detective he'd have me believe he was?'

'Detective! That's a good one! I don't know what Boyd is, honestly I don't, only my instincts tell me he isn't on the right side of the law, even if he's never been caught yet. Perhaps it's me – I just distrust a person who shies from work and is always borrowing and smart-talking his way in and out of things,' Julie said shortly.

'Yes, well, don't blame yourself. I knew that he was no good the last time he came to us, when you found him in the garden with me. I've thought about it all day today and I'd made up my mind to tell you, to warn you, even though he is your own cousin.'

'Warn me?' Julie whispered.

'Aye. When I catch someone out smart-talking about something, pretending they know all about it when I know they don't,

147

why then, I start thinking pretty sharp about 'em.'

'And you caught Boyd out?'

'I did. There's three things I know inside out: gardening,' he said, counting on the fingers of his left hand, 'and fishing, and what you might call being handy with electrics. There's not much you can tell me about fixing electric things, though I might not look like it. Taught myself, as a kind of a hobby, after my accident. I don't know much else besides them three things, but I know 'em well. And I caught your Boyd out on all three of 'em.'

'Oh!' Julie said, and subsided. Boyd didn't usually let himself get caught out, but he had made the mistake of under-rating Gideon Leigh's knowledge. He had been misled by that slow, inarticulate manner of Gideon's.

'Your Boyd started talking big about gardening. He made a mistake that stared me in the face. No use telling you what it was, lass, on account of you don't know about mulch and manures, *I* know!'

Julie smiled and shook her head.

'Now, it was a silly mistake he made. It wasn't a thing he could have read up in a book, because you wouldn't find it in a book. It's the sort of thing you'd only find out after a lifetime spent with the soil. He made out he was an expert spare-time gardener, and had information he could give *me* on the

148

subject. Now, when a chap makes that sort of mistake, I start watching out, and sure enough, he got something wrong when he was swanking about how much he knew about fishing–'

'Mr Leigh, he wants me to do something bad, I think. He hasn't told me what it is yet. He has only said he knows someone who would pay him to borrow the big collar on show in the shop, just to wear for one night, at a ball.'

Gideon stared at her, uncomprehending.

'That's the sort of thing Boyd does – helps people to get copies made of expensive pieces, and replaces them. He says he only wants information from someone who works inside, and then he laughed and said it wasn't me, because he knew I wouldn't give him information.'

'What are you *going* to do, lass?'

She spread her hands. 'I can't go to the police. It's only in my mind. I've no proof.'

'You haven't, have you?'

'But I just can't do nothing, and wait for it to happen and then find that everyone thinks it was me!'

'No, you can't do that.'

'Then what *can* I do? Don't tell me to start running again. He'll find me, eventually, because of going to the hospital. Unless … come to think of it, why do I have to attend a hospital anywhere? I'm getting used to this

149

limp. I don't believe in my heart that they'll ever be able to put it right. Where could I go, I wonder? Let me think?'

'You could go to Birmingham or Sheffield or Manchester or even Cardiff. No shortage of towns, big or little, to go to, lass, only I'm thinking it might be the better way to stay where you are and face it out.'

'How?' she cried in despair.

'Well, *I* believe you, so why shouldn't anyone else, provided they have a basinful of your Boyd and get their sights on him and weigh him up.'

'You're mixing your metaphors, darling Mr Leigh,' Julie said shakily.

'What I was thinking was, you're by way of being a friend of Mr Howe himself. Well, why not visit him and tell him what you've told me?'

'What could *he* do, from a hospital bed?'

'He might give an order on the quiet to change all the locks and alarm systems – money's no object to him – and he might give an order to have a watch kept in the shop at night.'

Julie shook her head. 'No, Boyd doesn't work like that. He isn't a jewel thief, he's a confidence man.' She whispered the last two words.

There, now it was out. Her secret fears over months, a lifetime, it seemed.

Gideon looked horrified. 'You knew it,

lass? Yet you go out with him, you acknowledge him?'

'I don't think I admitted it to myself before.
I don't think I realised it before. It's only
through talking to you, Mr Leigh, that's
made it all click into place. You see, there are
times when he teases me and does theoretical
"jobs" as he calls them. Impossible thefts,
just to make me say it couldn't be done. Now
I'm beginning to believe they have been
done, like that. Oh, not with Boyd doing the
job, but I think he may have had some part in
it, perhaps only thinking up the idea.'

'That don't let him off being guilty,'
Gideon said.

'I've no proof! There was one time when a
piece was in a case on show all the time,
night and day, with a light on. Well, no one
could bungle that set-up, but something
happened to it that looked like a natural
accident. Something heavy fell on to it,
smashing the case and damaging the piece.
It had to be taken out of its case and sent to
the workshop to be repaired, and while it
was out of its closely guarded case, it somehow got switched. No one knew when. It
was only discovered afterwards, when it went
to the customer, who said a copy had been
sent to her. At least, that was Boyd's theoretical story, to make me say it couldn't be
done.'

'He's a bit of a Tartar, isn't he?' Gideon

observed. 'Well, I reckon you ought to safe-guard yourself somehow, lass, by going and telling someone that you've got reason to believe someone's going to try and have a go at getting that collar thing.'

'How will I say I know? Who shall I say is going to do it – the elegant young man who came and bought expensive cuff-links, or his friend who lost his own valuable tie-pin in the shop and came back for it?'

'Yes, it's a bit ticklish. Still, if they are in the doubt you say they are, over that brace-let, well, they might listen to you. Say you were to tell them you heard someone talking about it? Well, you did, didn't you? You don't have to say who it was, do you?'

Julie shook her head. 'I don't know, I just don't know, Mr Leigh. Still, thanks for let-ting me get it out of my system.'

They walked back together, soberly. It was dark by the time they arrived. Vera scolded, and didn't entirely believe them when Julie asserted she had only just joined Mr Leigh at the gate, even though that was the actual truth, since she had stayed at the end of the street to give him a head start for that pur-pose. Vera had seen Julie come along on her own and join Gideon, but she was suspicious all the same. Those two, she considered, shared something, behind that still façade and the looks they sometimes exchanged.

Julie spent a sleepless night. She missed

going out with Adam unbelievably. Going out with Neville didn't do anything to assuage the loss, although her very aloofness intrigued Neville and made him more attentive than he might otherwise have been.

She lay there thinking about what Gideon had advised, using the thoughts to push away from her that last time she had seen Adam; the long look he had directed at her, and the way that look had reduced her to a shivering jelly. She was angry with herself; angry, frustrated, grief-stricken. If this was being in love, why had it to happen to her, when the man wasn't even free?

Next day she resolved to go up to Mr Howe and tell him enough to jolt him into putting the people in the shop on the alert. How she was going to do it, she had no idea. If she wasn't careful, she would arouse his suspicions to such an extent that he would suggest she gave up her job in the shop, as being a confidante of people likely to rob him. And she hadn't wanted to go near him again, because of the possibility of seeing Adam's wife again.

In the Appointments Office that morning Julie had to deal with a lot of Adam's cases. She saw him go in and once he came out with a house surgeon and they had stood talking for what seemed hours and she couldn't tear her eyes away from him. When she did, she found the clerk who had been talking of Adam's wife that day, looking at her very oddly indeed.

When she was free to go to her lunch, she hardly knew whether she would go and see Cedric Howe or not, but finally she did.

He wasn't in a very good mood. 'I'm glad you've come up, my dear,' the ward sister said kindly. 'He's been asking why you haven't been to see him lately.'

Julie nodded. 'I thought he might be. I hope I can cheer him up, or at least get him interested.' It would most likely be the latter result, she thought.

He growled at her when he saw who it was. 'I was just going to have my rest,' he bawled at her.

'Then I'll go,' Julie said.

'No, come back here, girl!' He indicated the chair by his bed. 'Sit down and tell me why you go to lunch so late. Can't be good for you!'

'I like it late. It suits me. Then someone can drive me back to Fleckbury.'

'Oh. Well, what have you been doing with yourself? Why haven't you been to see me lately?'

'I didn't think you'd want me to come every day,' she said helplessly, for want of some better excuse.

'Well, I do! That's if you're not bored with talking to the old fellow? Heh?'

'No, of course I'm not, and actually I came

154

today to ask your advice about something.'

'Ah!' He positively purred. He loved having his advice asked, and so few people did ask for it.

'What I wanted to know was, if I heard anything said that would lead me to think that the shop was going to be burgled, what would I do?' His frown made her add, 'For the best, I mean, because without proof, it wouldn't be any good going to the police, would it?'

'Is this a hypothetical question, or have you really heard something, m'dear?' he asked, but he was still frowning.

'I have heard something, but it was so vague, I can't tell you what made me think it might be real, but it would be very hard to convince anyone in authority that it wasn't just that silly game some people play, about how they would commit an impossible burglary and get away with it.'

'In this case, what impossible burglary was going to be committed, if only in theory?' he asked, with a comical lift of one eyebrow. 'I suppose it was your friends, at a party!'

She was so relieved to agree with him, that she was sure her relief would be patently obvious and arouse his suspicions.

'It was the Mendellini Collar, and it was a sort of theory exercise.'

'The Mendellini Collar,' he said, and then leaned forward to say impressively, 'that is a piece that no one in their right mind would want to take, because of it's being too distinctive, it would be marked in no time. "Hot", I believe, is the term. But,' he said, raising one hand as she started to speak, 'if some idiot did manage to get it from us, it would create such a scandal that it would be the end of the firm. We are a small fish in a small backwater,' he finished, smiling sadly. 'It wouldn't shake the nations, but it would do all the harm in the world to our local goodwill.'

'Oh, Mr Howe!' Julie exclaimed. 'I'm sure no one would take it, not really, but as I heard it talked of (you know, just as a joke!) and these jokes do sometimes come off, I felt I had to tell you. I don't want to worry you, but isn't there something you can personally authorise to be done, to guard against one of these silly jokes coming off?'

'You're a good girl, a good girl,' he said absently, patting her hand. 'Run along now, and I'll have a think.'

'You're sure you won't lie here and worry about it?' she said again.

'Run along, child, I'll be all right,' he insisted.

Julie was so worried about Cedric Howe that she forgot to be on the look-out for Adam Hollidge. She almost ran into him coming up the stairs.

'Julie! I've been trying to find you. They

said you were still in the hospital somewhere,' he said, taking her arm.

There was a side passage with a window at
the end. Julie didn't know where it led to,
but no one was in it, and Adam took her
down its length to the window with such
determination that she didn't dare to question him. He was somehow rather intimidating without his white coat, and in his black
jacket and pin-striped trousers. He had lost
that friendly look, too. At any other time she
might have read in his serious countenance
the signs of strain, but today she only saw
him as someone she ought to have watched
out for, avoided, because he was not for her
and she would betray herself. Angrily and
quite unreasoningly, she blamed Adam for
being there at all today, just when she had
been too worried about something else to
give him a thought.

'What did you want me for?' she asked,
unaware of how frosty her young voice
sounded.

'Do you remember that in the beginning
of this nice friendship of ours, we agreed to
let each other know if we couldn't be available any evening?'

She nodded.

'Well, I've kept my part of the bargain.
Couldn't you have let me know you were
going out with some chap in a fast car the
night before last?'

That, of course, was the night she had gone out with Neville Stannard.

As she didn't answer, he went on, rather grimly, 'I called for you, but I was just in time to see you both drive off. And last night I was too late to even get a sight of you.'

Last night. Julie remembered how worried she had been, after Boyd had brought her home. 'I only walked to the river to meet–' she began, and broke off before she had given Gideon's name, leaving Adam thinking quite naturally that it had been some other young man she had been going to the river to meet.

He nodded. 'To meet someone else. I know. I asked your landlady where you were, and she looked flustered and finished up by telling me rather loudly that you were out with your cousin. But we know, don't we, Julie, that your cousin was the one person you wished to avoid, not long ago. Or wasn't he? Were you just having me on, with that nice display of fear about a man looking in the window of the shop?'

'You asked my landlady? But she didn't mention you'd called!' Julie fumed.

'I should hope not. I impressed on her that I didn't want her to say anything about it.'

'Well, why, I should like to know! If you want to know who I was with last night, it was poor old Gideon, only we couldn't tell her, because she thinks it's sinful to sit

158

around talking. I had something I wanted advice on, and he seems to be the only really staunch friend I have!'

His eyebrows shot up angrily, but Julie rushed on, blindly, because she was unhappy and hurt and uncertain. 'You can look like that at me! It's all very fine! But it's true! You said you'd be my friend but I can't trust you like I can Gideon Leigh. You've got a nerve taking me up on going out with other people, but what else can you expect, if you don't act honest and straightforward with me! Letting me tell you how much I liked you, and making an ass of myself over it, and all that talk about us being friends, when all the time you're married! Yes, and everyone else but me knows you've got a wife because she's all over the hospital, pushing a beastly book trolley!'

CHAPTER NINE

Julie turned sharply away from him as she spoke, and put both hands up to her face, to prevent him from seeing how it was working and how her lips were trembling. To burst into tears now, here in this place, with him, would be too humiliating for words.

He gently turned her round and forced

her to look at him. She saw that his expression was one of alarm more than anything else.

'I didn't know she was here, Julie, believe me! I knew the Almoner, who is a friend of mine, was looking for something to keep Rosalind occupied, but I had no idea it was in this hospital.'

'That isn't the point,' she choked. 'I don't care where she works or who knows about it, so long as I do! Can't you see how awful it is, with people breaking off talking about her and nudging each other because I'm within earshot? You see what they think about me – the sort of girl who goes out with a married man.'

'Oh, what a lot of rot, Julie. Oh, let's get out of here. Let's find somewhere private to discuss this.'

'There's nothing to discuss, Mr Hollidge,' she said stiffly, anger giving her a degree of control as nothing else could. 'Whatever you may think, and however your other patients behave, I'm not the sort of girl to be friends with a man without his wife knowing, and I'm surprised that you would think I was.'

Following that outburst, it went very quiet. She was aware of a couple of sparrows fighting on the window-sill over a few crumbs that someone had thrown out. Beyond the end of the corridor, she could hear the lift whining up, its doors clanging open and shut, and whining down again. Few people used the stairs, and if there was anyone in the rooms off this corridor, they must be either deaf and dumb or thoroughly enjoying this emotional scene.

Suddenly Adam said, in a quiet, rather broken voice, 'I know that, Julie. I just didn't think of it like that. You were all alone, so you said, and you seemed so scared, I didn't think of anything else except to help you. And then you grew on me, and the only important thing was to keep your friendship. As to mentioning Rosalind, well, I don't. I hardly think of myself as married, anyway, and I'm sure she doesn't think of herself as my wife. She's Gregory's patient, and she's been away in a Home for so long–'

He broke off and shrugged. Now the tired lines, the lines of strain, were so much marked in his face that even Julie couldn't fail to notice them.

'Now you seem to have gathered some young friends round you, and no one is more glad than I. I can turn you over to them. But don't worry about people thinking the wrong things about you – they won't. They know how I take up my patients and thrust my spare time on them. You may even have their sympathy, on the grounds of it being an occupational hazard on the part of the unsuspecting patients of the eccentric Adam Hollidge.' And he even managed to call up a small rueful smile to take any sting out of those words.

It tore at Julie. She wanted to fling her arms round him and tell him that she didn't really mind what people said about her, so long as she could believe that he cared a little about her, and that she could help him in some way as he had been helping her.

She didn't, of course. She stared at him, stunned. She realised that he himself was terminating that nice friendship, not giving her a chance to rail at him any more. She was going to lose him, definitely, finally. She would have to be formal with him when he examined that leg of hers in future. Blot out of her mind the memory of the lake and the small craft on it, and the pleasant anticipation of such other times to come. Only then did she realise how much she had come to depend on that warm friendship with him, of such a short duration. But it had never, of course, really belonged to her.

'Come along. Want to be given a lift anywhere, or shouldn't I make the offer?' he said, in a rallying tone.

She shook her head, in a dazed way. 'No, I – I probably shan't be coming to the hospital any more – I might be leaving the town. I don't know. I would like–'

'But Julie, you can't just leave when we're on the verge of doing something for you! Where will you go?'

'To Wales,' she said, without having given the matter any thought at all. It popped into her head. Her birthplace. 'I was born there. It seems logical to want to go back. I always have hankered to return. Well, I will now. Why not? Anyway, I shan't be having any more hospital treatment. It's no use trying to persuade me – I don't believe there's any hope, and if I don't believe, how can anyone help me?'

He let her go then. She could feel his eyes following her limping away, and she couldn't stop herself from stumbling occasionally. It was always the way when she was flurried or upset, this leg played her up, it acted as if it wasn't one of her own limbs, no part of her person, but something strange and alien she was dragging behind her. It made her feel so wretched, she just wanted to sit down and weep, there on the stairs.

Only the sight of an orderly carrying a tray up, stopped her from such a course. She went down sedately, and kept on thinking that what with this row with Adam and the trouble over that Mendellini Collar, it was high time she moved on, and the chances were that Boyd would never dream she would go back to the village where she had been born. She talked hard to herself, telling herself she would make a series of train and bus journeys, doubling back and forth, to make it difficult for Boyd to trace her, and with a bit of luck she might evade him.

She called out to the clerk she knew in the Appointments Office: 'Who's going to take me back to Fleckbury today, Joan?'

'No one today, dear – a handsome young man has turned up for you in his car! Aren't you the lucky one!'

Handsome young man! That description could only fit Neville, who was, so far as she knew, the only young man with a car who knew her movements at the hospital each day. She went through to the front with mixed feelings. For perhaps the first time, she would be glad to see Neville. He was at least neutral.

Rosalind Osborne joined her. She slouched along, her hair untidy, her make-up needing replenishing, her hands in her jacket pockets. Although her clothes had once been good, she somehow contrived to make them look tawdry, cheap, and far from new or clean, and she didn't seen to care.

'Hi,' she said to Julie. 'Mind if I tag along? I heard them say you had transport. That's what I could do with.'

'But I'm going to Fleckbury, and it isn't hospital transport,' Julie warned her.

'It's okay by me, chum. Wherever you're going, and whatever you're going in, that's okay by me. All I ask is that you drop me off at the first hostelry.'

Remembering what the ambulance driver

had said to Rosalind Osborne on that other occasion, Julie said, 'But I can't do that – you know I can't!'

'Ah, go on! Just because you heard Bert say what he did you don't have to be that way too, honey. Besides, I'm on the wagon. They wouldn't let me out if I wasn't.'

Julie wished she would go away, but there was no law against Rosalind's walking beside anyone she chose, Julie supposed. And after all, she was Adam's wife.

'Well, why do you want to be dropped off at such places, then, if you're really not – not–'

Rosalind grinned lopsidedly. 'Ah, I see you know my sad story, or you wouldn't boggle at saying the naughty word "drink". Shame! Who told you? Don't answer that– I can guess. As I like to go in a pub for the company, and because it's the only place I know that serves a decent hot meal without a lot of argument from dreary creatures in waitresses uniforms, who just love to make me wait for my food. No, give me a pub any old time. Now, here we are – and which bit of transport is for you, honey?'

Julie looked round and saw, to her intense despair, that it wasn't Neville waiting for her, but Boyd. Boyd in a brand-new shiny black limousine that at first she couldn't believe.

'Julie! Look, love, how do you like the new

165

buggy?' he shouted, getting out and coming over to her at a run. 'Come on, sweetie, been waiting ages for you.'

'How did you know what time I'd be coming out?' Julie asked him, unhappily aware that Rosalind Osborne was still at her side, taking all this in, so Julie couldn't let herself be candid with him.

'Old Gideon let on,' Boyd said, grinning unashamedly, and then his glance slid round to Rosalind. 'Introduce me to your friend, love – where are your manners?'

'Rosalind Osborne – Boyd Markwick,' Julie said shortly, not caring that she had made the introduction in such a way. How could he? How could that Osborne creature hang about, waiting to butt in?

'I've seen you before – now where? On the stage!' Boyd said, a nice note of admiration mixed with awe in his voice. It was a well-worn line, but apparently Rosalind wasn't proof against it. She looked pleased.

'Someone remembers me. Three cheers!' she jeered softly at herself.

Of course, in no time at all, Boyd had presumed that Rosalind was free to try out the new car as well as Julie was. Julie sat in the back, with Rosalind beside Boyd. They left the hospital grounds in fine style, narrowly missing an ambulance, and ripped out on to the motorway, in spite of Julie's protesting that she just wanted to go back to

Fleckbury as soon as possible.

She was late getting to the shop, in spite of forgoing her lunch. Hungry, tired and cross, she explained to Mr Gooch that she had spent rather longer with Mr Howe that day than usual, and that she had been delayed in getting back.

She didn't care whether Mr Gooch were satisfied or not. She was desperately worried about Boyd and that car, and far from satisfied with his explanation that a friend had bought it new and left it to him to run in. She was far from sure that any good would come of Rosalind Osborne's interest in Boyd, and quite certain that she herself shouldn't have left Rosalind in the car with him, without somehow warning him of her history and who she really was. But how could she have done such a thing, she asked herself? There had been no opportunity. Boyd had wanted to be alone with Rosalind, that was clear, by the alacrity he had shown in running Julie back to the shop after he had been showing off the car's points for such a little while.

She was very upset about Adam, too, and that painful scene she had had in the hospital corridor with him. What on earth would Adam have to say, if he found out that his wife had met Boyd through Julie, and had shown such an interest in his company?

She was also far from happy about the

state in which she had left old Cedric Howe, after having told him as much as she dared about the danger in which she believed the Mendellini Collar to be in.

Heavens above, she thought, as she did her best to satisfy an elderly lady with an acid tongue and slender purse, who had come in for something nice, as she put it, to give to an old friend, without much idea of what she wanted – heavens above, why did things have to so wrong all of a sudden? It wasn't so long since she had been congratulating herself on having found a peaceful place like Fleckbury in which to ease out after the trying time she had had in London. Now, with the arrival of Boyd, everything had deteriorated, and it was just as worrying and impossible.

Neville came over to her counter just before tea-time. She thought he must be going to take her out to tea again, and she tried to marshal her thoughts: should she tell him what she had told his uncle? And while she struggled to come to a decision, Mr Wexibole came and called Neville back into the inner office to take an important and private telephone call.

She went to her tea alone, and thought over again the things she had told Mr Howe. What steps would he take from his hospital bed, to prevent Boyd and his friends from trying out any of their schemes, supposing they were really going to? Or would old Cedric Howe just lie there in bed fretting and worrying about it, unable to decide on a course which he himself could usefully take?

Her fears were put at rest when she went back to the shop. There was a flap on, round the glass case which contained the Mendellini Collar. It was being taken out, and conveyed to the inner office. A little later on, Neville Stannard went through with the big leather case in which expensive pieces were conveyed. Mr Gooch went with him to his car.

Julie eased out, and almost smiled broadly with happiness to think that that horrid piece of jewellery had been removed from the shop. Old Mr Howe must have telephoned to his nephew to tell him to take it away. Julie didn't care whether it had been taken to the old man's home or to Neville's place or the bank or a strong-room. The main point was that it had been removed from the show-case in the shop, and out of Boyd's reach.

Charlie Carr had something to say about it.

'That's a fine carry-on, if you like!'

Julie looked at him with disfavour. 'What is?'

'Old Stannard taking that precious piece out of the case and driving himself with it. You'd think he'd take someone else with him! Why, he might get held up by gunmen or something – that's worth a lot of money, between ourselves.'

'Where is he taking it?' Julie asked fear-fully.

'That's the queer thing about it. Old Wexi-bole was telling old Gooch that that Ackery girl telephoned to ask for it to be sent over for her Daddy to see it. Wants to give it to her old auntie for a present, if old auntie likes it.'

Julie's hand flew to her throat. 'Miss Ackery asked for it? Are you sure?'

'You really are a disbelieving little madam, aren't you?' Charlie complained. 'I don't know why I bother to give you these tit-bits of news, when I stick my neck out to get 'em red-hot and fresh with my very own ears, jammed to the key-hole. I heard him talk to her on the phone about it!'

'I don't believe you,' Julie said hotly. 'She wouldn't ask for it – she's seen the thing and she hated it.'

'Ah, but old auntie might like it!'

'Then why didn't her old aunt come to the shop?'

'Perhaps she's the old aunt who's in a wheel-chair and never comes out, but if she's as rich as I've heard she is, then she could afford a couple of Mendellini Collars,' Charlie grinned.

'You were only fooling about him being

170

held up though, weren't you? I mean, who would know what he'd got in that case? Anyway, no one would try to steal the Mendellini Collar – it's too well-known, isn't it? I mean, they couldn't sell it again.'

'You don't read your detective novels closely,' Charlie told her. 'What you do is first to find someone willing to break it down, melt the setting and dig out the gems. Then you find someone who'll buy the stones, and Bob's your uncle. All these chaps know a fence and a customer before they pinch the article. Don't you believe that stuff about no one wanting to handle "hot" pieces. They go in for the fun of the thing.' He groaned. 'Cavey – here comes old Gooch!'

Julie was glad that Mr Gooch kept such a strict eye on her, because it meant that the tiresome Charlie Carr couldn't spend too much time at her counter talking to her. Yet he had stayed long enough to drop some seeds of doubt into her new-found peace of mind. She was glad when it was time to go home.

She dawdled on the way. Tonight she had no spirit left to combat the home-going queues for the buses and for perhaps the first time for a long while, there was no one to take her to Canary Lane in a car. Neville hadn't come back to the shop, Boyd was presumably still out with Rosalind Osborne, and Adam had, in effect, said good-bye to her today.

It was well after six by the time she painfully limped up the path of No 16.

There was no one in the garden, either, and without the sight of Gideon to welcome her with his inarticulate pleasure, everything seemed suddenly very dreary.

He came out of the kitchen as he heard her open the door, and for once he wasn't inarticulate.

'Is that you, Julie, lass? We've just been listening to the News – one of the people at your shop has copped it.'

She stopped dead in her tracks, her heart beating uncomfortably fast. 'What did you say, Mr Leigh?' she asked, in a strained, unnatural voice.

'Yes, that's right – chap named Neville Stannard.'

'Neville! What happened to him?' she gasped, thinking at once of what Charlie Carr had said.

'He was in a mix-up on that corner that they keep saying needs traffic lights. Perhaps they'll put 'em there now. It always needs an accident to get something done.'

'But what happened to him?' she persisted. 'Is he–'

'Now, now, you look quite white, lass. Sorry if I said it in too much of a rush. Here, come and sit down. I forgot for the moment that he's a friend of yours.'

172

'Tell her, for goodness sake, that he's all right!' Vera said wrathfully. 'Just a bit shook up. He's been taken to the hospital, of course, and like as not he'll be kept there for a day or two, but it was his car that got messed up. Now what are you looking like that for? I said he's all right, didn't I?'

Julie's legs gave way and she sat down suddenly. 'How did it happen?' she asked, licking her dry lips. 'Does anyone know yet?'

'Well, they didn't say much on the News. Seems like they were more interested about the need for traffic lights, and this here accident pushing things that way, it seemed to me,' Gideon said. 'But Ben Horrocks next door happened to be near enough to get a look in, about that time, and he said it was so unnecessary, really. Just a flipping mix-up between a learner driver, a chap with a crossing-sweeper bin on wheels, and your pal in his car, and if he'd been looking about him he could have pulled up in time, but he goes and brakes too sharp-like and skids right across the road into a lamp standard.'

'I must go and see him,' Julie said. 'I'll never sleep if I don't.'

Vera and Gideon exchanged blank glances. Julie knew they were thinking they had been wrong about her and Boyd, and that they were now scenting a romance between her and Neville Stannard.

173

She had to let them go on thinking that. So far as Adam was concerned, it didn't matter now what anyone thought about her. Adam wasn't likely to have any contact with the Leighs, and if he heard about her interest in Neville, perhaps it would be a good thing, anyway.

But for herself, all Julie wanted was to find out what had happened to that ill-fated piece of jewellery, the Mendellini Collar. She had to satisfy herself that, incredible as it seemed, it had nothing to do with Boyd, this accident to Neville, who was supposed to be carrying the thing out of harm's way. To that end, she told herself as she pulled on her raincoat and grabbed up her handbag, she must see them all: not only Neville, but old Mr Howe, Boyd himself if necessary. But she had to know what was going on, and if that piece of jewellery was still safe.

CHAPTER TEN

Neville Stannard was asleep. 'I don't think I'd disturb him now if I were you,' the ward sister said. She knew Julie. 'But if you really want to visit someone, what about his uncle? You do go and see Mr Howe some-times, I believe?'

Julie nodded. 'But before I see him, I ought to be briefed on how much he knows about this, oughtn't I?'

'He knows, I'm afraid. He heard the news, but he took it very well when we told him his nephew was only badly shaken up. I'm afraid he took rather a malicious pleasure in pointing out that his nephew was not a really responsible driver.'

Julie detected again that joyous amusement they all felt for old Cedric Howe.

'There was the question of a leather case,' she said hesitantly. 'It contained jewellery. I thought Mr Stannard was taking it to his uncle's home, but I later heard that it was going to a customer.'

'Yes, we have heard about that, too,' the ward sister agreed. 'The press have had to be allowed in, and the police, but everything is being done to recover them.'

Julie felt sick. 'You mean, the case had gone? It had been stolen?'

'Well, it wasn't in the wreckage of the car, but perhaps someone will find it. After all, no one would know there was anything of value in it, would they, dear?'

Julie shivered. 'No, I suppose not. I don't quite know how it happened.'

'Well, from the moment of collision to the time of taking the car away, the police were on the spot,' the ward sister said reasonably. 'Now, you trot along to Mr Howe's room and cheer him up. Oh, and perhaps you'd better not tell him the case isn't to be found, in case he worries. I'll speak to Sister Mecklin over the phone and warn her you're coming.'

They were all taking it so casually. Of course, in this place no one would know the significance of the Mendellini Collar, Julie supposed wretchedly.

She went down to Mr Howe's room but there was an Engaged ticket on the door. One of the nurses told her that a Mr Gooch was with Mr Howe.

That was it, then, Julie told herself. Mr Gooch would of course have heard about the loss of the case, and he wouldn't have had the wit to keep it from his chief. But on second thoughts, it was Mr Gooch's duty, in the absence of Neville, to go to the head of the firm. There would be descriptions to give to the police, and there would be the insurance people to see, and heaven knew what. What, too, would Dian Ackery be thinking? She had asked to have the thing brought to her aunt, to be looked at.

Julie went out of the hospital again, but now she had no clear idea what to do or where to go. Boyd had told her where he was staying, but she hadn't got the actual address, and she didn't know where she could telephone him. There was, of course, Wyndham Fox. She did know where he lived, but of what use telephoning him? He wouldn't know her needs: he wouldn't appreciate how vital it was to get hold of Boyd, and if Boyd didn't want her to find him ... if they were both in it together...

Now more than at any other time, Julie was sure she knew what Boyd was up to. Somehow he had engineered this thing, so that he could take the Collar. How he had persuaded Neville to believe that Dian had wanted to see it, Julie couldn't say, but she was certain in her heart that Boyd was at the bottom of the theft. After all, he had made friends with Dian that day – supposing he had somehow talked her into wanting to see that piece of jewellery, so that it could be got out of the shop? But then, Julie argued to herself, her heart beating faster every minute, but then that would mean that Boyd was also the author of that accident, and that would be wicked. He couldn't possibly have relied on coincidence, could he?

No, the whole thing was too fantastic. The case must have been lost somehow and it would turn up again ... if it weren't found by someone who would know its value and who wasn't honest enough to return it.

Perhaps because of her unwillingness to believe that Boyd could do such a wicked thing as this, she decided to refrain from making any effort to get into touch with him at all.

As she left the gates of the hospital she

thought she could hear someone calling her. Blind panic set in, and although she couldn't run, the same fear that led her to think it was the police or press wanting to question her, endowed her limbs with the ability to twist and turn into this side street and that, and even though she didn't hurry by normal standards, she made a good enough speed to get her out of earshot of whoever wanted her.

Finally her feet took her to the river, the same spot where she had sat and talked to Gideon Leigh.

Instinctively she sat there, huddling her coat round her, staring at the water and wishing Gideon would come, to comfort her, her offer her sound advice.

When a man's footsteps did come slowly along the path behind the boat-house, she leapt up with Gideon's name on her lips, but it wasn't Gideon.

It was Adam Hollidge.

'You!' she whispered. 'What are *you* doing here?'

'I called you, Julie, as you left the hospital, but you wouldn't wait for me, so I followed you. What on earth is the matter, my dear? You're white as a sheet.'

Any ears were better than none, so she said flatly, 'If you want to know, I thought it was the police after me. The most awful thing's happened. Neville Stannard was taking the Mendellini Collar to a customer and he got into a crash and the thing's lost and he's in the hospital and I don't know what to do.'

He stood leaning, one foot on the step above the one she was sitting on, his elbow on that knee. Leaning over her, near enough to touch her but not touching her. She couldn't bear him being so near, yet his being near had a certain bitter sweetness about it, that at least quelled her fears, and gave her a transitory sense of security.

'How does it concern you, Julie?' he asked quietly.

'Well, you see, it does, doesn't it? I mean, all that has happened, about Boyd and all that—'

'Tell me about it, from the very beginning,' he invited. 'Don't leave anything out.'

With only the sound of the water lapping at their feet, and the jarring sound of a bird, disturbed into making a raucous call from the bushes nearby, Julie settled down to telling him; quietly, without fuss, leaving nothing out.

'Have you any proof that he really does anything criminal, or is he just a young tearaway, putting up a show to impress you?' Adam asked at last.

'I wish I knew,' Julie said sombrely. 'How does he live? *I* don't know. Sometimes he borrows money, from me – from anyone who'll lend it to him – but there are other times when he seems pretty flush, but I never hear how. You see, I get an uneasy feeling about the way he talks. Surely he wouldn't talk about how things *can* be taken, without meaning to take them? On the other hand,' she ruminated, clearly trying to persuade herself, 'he might just be talking big to make me think he is on the wrong side of the law and getting away with it, when all the time he's making money by legitimate means.'

'You think he goes out to work and is ashamed to let you know he's so ordinary after all the big talk?'

'Oh, no, I don't think that of Boyd, but it did just occur to me that he might make money at the races sometimes. He wouldn't mind doing that, whereas work – well, I don't think he's ever held a job down.'

'What about the old fellow in the bookshop who got killed in your accident? What were the findings at the inquest?' Adam pursued.

Julie had been hoping against hope that that would not come up. She had never been happy about that herself. She had often meant to take steps to find out what the verdict had been, but that would have drawn attention to herself, she had always thought. And Boyd had been so definite about it.

'I was still too ill in hospital – the police did

180

come and ask questions but I wasn't there at the inquest–' she said, in a breathless rush.

'But there must have been a definite verdict, Julie, and you must have seen newspapers – afterwards, if not at the time.'

'Boyd told me about it,' she said. 'Boyd hinted that some friends of his (you know I told you they were following him) saw it happen and said the old man had run out into the road and it was his fault. Boyd said the verdict had been accidental death.'

'But you told me it was Boyd's fault for grabbing the wheel and sending you into a spin. Now which is it, my dear? You can't have it both ways.'

'What good is it doing, speculating on that?' she cried wildly. 'I don't know exactly how it happened – only how I think it did, but I'm not really clear about it. I only know that if Boyd hadn't asked me for the lift that day, I wouldn't have been near Reuben's shop front and he would be alive now.' She choked and said, 'You wanted to know what Boyd does by way of a living, not whether he caused Reuben Floy to be killed.'

'No. I don't want to know anything of the sort,' Adam said sharply. 'All I want to know is how you personally stand in all this. Heavens, how I wish I were free to take the whole thing in hand, sort it all out, get at the truth behind all this vagueness. I'm a practical person, my dear. I do so dislike all this surmising and guesswork and instinct and all the things you seem to deal in. Julie, let me engage a friend of mine to help sort this out – a solicitor.'

'You can't.'

'You mean you don't want me to lift a finger to help you, not even through a third party, because I'm not free?'

'That's right. I don't want you to. I was going out of your life tonight – I would have been on the train now, if all this hadn't come up. I felt I had to see Neville, because I knew he had the Collar with him when he left the shop, and old Mr Howe is a friend of mine and I didn't want him to be bothered. I would have given the world not to have to see you again tonight. Don't you understand?'

'Julie, what are you trying to say?' he asked huskily.

He put out his hands to her, but she evaded him, and in doing so, she slipped. She would have fallen back into the river if he hadn't grasped her and held her.

She fell against him, shivering and sobbing, holding on to him as if for life itself, and he held her to him as if he would never let her go. She could feel his cheek pressing on the top of her head.

They stood there for a full minute. She could hear his heart thudding beneath his jacket. She thought he must be deafened by the beating of her own.

And then he put her from him. 'Come on, let me drive you to my mother's. It's just occurred to me – she'll know what to do.'

'No! You can't do that! Whatever would your mother think?' Julie gasped.

'I've told her a few things about you already. I daresay she thinks I'm just running true to form, getting acutely interested in another patient. She won't think it at all odd, I promise you.'

Adam lived in a big house lying well back from the road, just outside of Fleckbury. The tall peak of St Agnes's Hill brooded like a purple shadow over the woods at the end of the property, and made the view from the big picture windows of Mrs Hollidge's lounge look more like a painted backcloth than a garden. It was all too perfect for Julie's taste. The lawns were so smooth and velvety, with sharply cut edges, and the flower gardens were small and cut in fancy shapes in the grass. There was an oval pool that made Gideon's effort seem decidedly home-made, and the fountain really worked.

Mrs Hollidge seemed a little like her garden at first sight; too perfect. She couldn't possibly have looked like this, so well-groomed and (as Vera would have put it) ready for company, without knowing whom Adam was bringing home.

After the first ten minutes, however, Julie

revised her opinion. Mrs Hollidge was smooth and self-confident outside, but warm and understanding under the veneer. 'My dear, just leave it to my son. He's wonderful at fixing things,' she said, when she had heard the very brief outline of the story from Adam. 'You go off and make that telephone call to the hospital, dear,' she said to him. 'The message came through almost an hour ago, so it's time you did something about it. Meantime, I'd like to talk to Julie.'

When he had gone out of the room, Mrs Hollidge asked, 'Now, my dear, how old are you?'

It was blunt, with a change of manner; a change that suggested nothing more than that now the men were out of the room, so to speak, the women could take their back hair down without fear.

'Twenty-two,' Julie said.

'And how long have you known my son?'

'Not very long. I've only just found out that he's married. I was going away, actually, only all this stopped me. He came after me. I did try to get away, but this leg of mine drags. He found me by the old boat-house and made me tell him all about this.'

'I see. You're in love with my son, aren't you?'

Julie couldn't answer that in so many words. She just looked at Mrs Hollidge, agony in her eyes.

'Now look here, my dear, suppose some-one could get you out of this mess – and I don't see why they shouldn't! Where would you go?'

'You think I didn't mean it, that I was going away under my own steam?' Julie said faintly.

'I think that you need another woman to help you to get settled somewhere else with-out it looking as if you were leaving in a hurry,' Mrs Hollidge said firmly. 'What can you do?'

'Serve in a shop – type – drive a car. No, not any more, not with this limp. I forgot,' Julie said miserably.

'Well, it so happens that I believe I know the very person who would be delighted with your services, only you and I will keep it a secret. She's elderly, and wants someone to write her letters for her, deal with all her charities, read to her, do her personal shopping and keep her company, and as she has a rooted objection to people rushing about, I believe you would do very well. She's generous with the salary she pays, too. Now let me see – how soon would you be able to leave your present job?'

'I was intending to leave at once, and pay them a week's wages in lieu of notice,' Julie said with dignity.

'What about the place where you are stay-ing?'

Julie looked distressed again. She didn't want to run out on the Leighs, who had been kind to her, but she supposed she could give them the same termination. After all, she paid them in advance, and she was paid up until the end of the following week. She nodded her head.

'Very well, I'll write to my old friend at once, and it shall all be settled only – and this is one of the conditions, I'm afraid – I don't want you to see my son again. Oh, don't worry about the hospital angle – there is a fine hospital in the nearest town to where you are going.'

'Where would that be, Mrs Hollidge?'

'In Carlisle,' Adam's mother said blandly, beginning to write notes.

Carlisle. She couldn't have named a further destination if she'd tried, Julie thought, despairing. Still, it was no further away than her native Wales, and it was doubtful if Boyd would think of going to Carlisle to find her.

'I expect my son went straight back to the hospital, so that's all right,' Mrs Hollidge said, with satisfaction. 'I can drive you back to your lodgings in my car.'

But just then Adam came into the room, looking pleased.

'Now, what are you two girls hatching?' he began, rubbing his hands. 'Great news, Julie! First of all, after I'd telephoned the hospital, I thought of a friend of mine who can help us get to the bottom of all this non-sense on the part of your cousin Boyd – and between ourselves, I should like to know a little more about it, after what I've heard from the hospital.'

'Adam, really, it wasn't necessary–' his mother began, but he waved her to silence with an even broader smile.

'No, wait, mother, till you hear – they've just told me at the hospital that that wretched Mendellini Collar has turned up! Yes, it's found! A small child brought it in – the police have had it despatched to Stannard for him to look at and make sure it's all right. You can't take it in, can you, Julie? It's back, in its case, safe and sound.'

CHAPTER ELEVEN

Julie was dumbfounded. 'But I don't under-stand.'

'Apparently the leather case was thrown clear when the car crashed, and some child-ren picked it up and they've been playing with it, but an older boy heard on the radio that there was a reward being offered for it, so he had the bright idea of turning it in to the police.'

Julie's legs were shaking again. She couldn't

believe that this was the truth. Something, she felt instinctively, was wrong somewhere.

Mrs Hollidge wasn't going to allow anyone to waste time in idle speculation. 'Yes, well, that's perfectly splendid, and we're all very pleased, but shouldn't you be going to the hospital, dear?'

'All in good time, mother. I'll drive you home first, Julie, and on the way I'll tell you what I've said to my friend on the telephone. You've nothing to worry about—'

'Of course she hasn't, and anyway, I'm going to drive her home. It's all arranged, so you needn't be bothered, Adam,' his mother said. 'Come along, Julie. We've a lot to do.'

'Just a minute, Mother, what are you up to?'

'Julie tells me she is going away, and she needs another woman to help her. Don't interfere, Adam.'

'Yes, I know all about Julie's mad idea of going back to Wales, but that's the first place Markwick would look for her in, and anyway, I want her here. Fisher will want to talk to her, and anyway, Jancy's got a theory about the nerves of that right leg. He wants to examine her again.'

Mrs Hollidge looked at Julie in such a way that Julie knew she must insist on leaving, if she wanted help from this woman.

'I'm going away, Adam. I've got a new job,' Julie said, 'and it isn't in Wales, and I don't want to be examined any more. I have told you that already, haven't I?'

Mrs Hollidge winced at Julie's use of her son's Christian name, but before she could say anything, the front door banged, and Rosalind slouched past.

She stopped at the open door of the lounge and stared in at them all, her glance coming back to Julie. 'Hello, chum,' she said, 'I didn't know you were on calling terms in this house, heaven help you!'

'That will do, Rosalind,' Mrs Hollidge said in a nettled tone, 'and for goodness' sake go up and get a bath and do something to your hair. It looks terrible.'

'And I feel terrible,' Rosalind said cheerfully. 'But I like your Boyd, chum. He really lets a car rip, but he hasn't seen anything yet. Don't tell him I said so.'

'You know Boyd Markwick?' Mrs Hollidge asked faintly.'

'Mama-in-law, you do not keep your little eyes open,' Rosalind said playfully. 'And you do not really know whether you are coming or going,' and with her finger to the side of her nose in a knowing gesture, Rosalind weaved her way out of the room, singing softly to herself.

'Oh, no,' Mrs Hollidge moaned. 'She *hasn't* been–'

'Of course she hasn't, mother,' Adam said impatiently. 'She's just pretending, to tease you. Mother, I've been standing right next to her – I would have known, wouldn't I?'

'All right, Adam, dear, if you say so,' Mrs Hollidge agreed, but she looked suddenly ill and strained. Julie was sorry for her. She was only trying to help her son in a difficult position, but Adam wasn't the type to like anyone else to fight his battles for him. Julie wondered just what the stresses were in this house.

'Go and wait in my car, Julie, I want to talk to my mother for a minute,' Adam said.

'But I'm going to drive her,' his mother began.

'Julie!' Adam insisted, so she quietly limped out. His car was waiting in the drive where he had left it. She tugged at the door, but he had locked it, and forgotten.

It started to rain, so Julie went back to the house, intending to ask him for the key of the car.

She had left the lounge door open behind her when she went out and no one had shut it. Rosalind was standing at the foot of the stairs, hugging the banisters and laughing softly to herself at what she could hear.

'–and you'd let her go – you'd send Julie – to that horrible old Miss Kemp to run her off her feet, with her leg in the state it is? Mother, how *could* you?'

'No, Adam, Miss Kemp wouldn't hurt Julie, if I asked her not to run her about. Miss

Kemp is so badly in need of a companion that she'd agree to anything, I'm sure she would!'

'Yes, she'd agree to anything, to get someone,' Adam said bitterly, 'but what would happen after that? Mother, you can't solve things by sending people away. You tried it with Rosalind, and now you're trying it with Julie.'

'Only to save you and your career, my dear,' his mother moaned. 'You don't seem to realise how you're throwing yourself away, Adam. You stayed in this small place because of that unfortunate marriage–'

Rosalind had stopped her quiet laughter, and was just standing there, listening. Julie thought it was time to put a stop to it all.

She limped into the room and held her hand out to Adam. 'If you'll give me the car key, I'll go and sit in it, and in case you haven't realised it, this isn't a very private conversation,' and she looked significantly at the staircase.

There was no one there. Rosalind must have fled silently upstairs when she saw Julie go towards that room. Julie shrugged and limped out to the car.

Adam followed her soon afterwards.

'What can I say?' he asked despairingly, as he drove her out of the drive and into the quiet country road. 'This seemed the best place to bring you, but even my mother–'

'You haven't an idea, have you?' Julie burst out in exasperation. 'For such a sensible man you do the oddest things! What did you expect your mother to do – welcome another girl into her home when she's already saddled with a daughter-in-law like that? What did you expect me to feel when I realised that Rosalind Osborne is living in your home? I don't know where I expected her to live – I never gave it a thought – but honestly I didn't expect to see her there of all places!'

'Did you mind?' Clearly it wasn't of importance to him. The main thing in his mind was doing something to Julie's leg, and next in importance came the tricky problem of her safety, getting her away from Boyd whom she feared. Julie saw that, in a flash. She realised, perhaps for the first time, how little Rosalind meant to him, and how little Rosalind cared about him. Two people tolerating each other, because of the tragic twist their lives had taken.

'No, I don't really, I suppose, not now I'm out of it. It was embarrassing, though. Your mother looked so – so–' She broke off, because to continue would mean admitting what his mother had guessed and said about her own feelings for Adam. But he wasn't listening.

'What will you do now? Where shall I take you, Julie? I'd give the world to be free to reorganise your life, but I suppose, having had time to consider me in all my doubtful aspects, you wouldn't want it to be me doing the reorganising?'

She looked at him in amazement. 'If you don't know, there doesn't seem much sense in trying to answer that question,' she said at last. 'And I'd just like to be dropped at the end of Canary Lane.'

'No, at this time of night I shall see you personally to your door. What were you doing in the hospital, anyway?'

'I told you – I went to see Neville Stannard.'

'What, specially? I know you said you wanted to talk to him and to his uncle about that necklace, but are you sure it wasn't for any other reason, Julie? Don't be afraid to tell me if you like the fellow specially. You ought to have someone of your very own, you know.'

He was regretting his friendship with her, she thought; regretting that moment when he had held her to him, by the side of the river tonight. She was just another lame duck patient that he was anxious to get cured and settled.

'Look, pull in to the side, will you?' Julie asked him. They were getting too near to Canary Lane, and she didn't want to sit and talk to him outside. The less the Leighs knew about this, the less they could speculate; nice as Gideon was, he wouldn't understand her friendship with Adam, if he, like everyone else, knew that Adam was married.

Adam needed no second bidding. He slid smoothly into a lay-by intended for buses. This section of the road wasn't very well lit, and the hourly bus on this route had only just gone. It was quiet, the rain steady now, making a regular drum-drumming on the roof of the car. What lights there were, reflected themselves in the wet road ahead like long spears of yellow, and the trees soughing in the wind, weaved patterns all over them. Now that the engine was shut off, she could think, and she had so much to think about, and quickly.

'Don't interrupt me, please. There are some things I have to say – now. At this moment. First of all, I want to leave Fleckbury. Please – let me explain why. It's been spoilt for me from the first, because in the beginning I kept looking over my shoulder, expecting Boyd to be there, and then he was there and interfered with everything I'd tried to build up for myself – my job, my landlady and her husband, my little life in this place. Well, I want to get away, start somewhere else, where there's a hope that he won't find me. He's poison to me wherever he goes.'

'But you won't shake him off by running away, Julie.'

'That's what Gideon tells me, but neither of you understand. I've had him on my back

194

for most of my life. I'm too used to his ways, to have any philosophy about him. To get free of him – that's all I want. Well, the Collar's back, so that worry's gone, but you've stopped up my one sure retreat – the job your mother knew of. Now I want you to tell her I still need her help, and I don't want you to interfere. You don't know how I shall get on with that old person your mother knows. She might just suit me, for all you know!'

He sat very still, thinking. The windscreen wiper was playing back and forth, very quickly, and watching it Julie felt mesmerised, sleepy. She shut her eyes so she shouldn't see it, but it was drawing towards the end of the day and she was tired, desperately tired.

She had no idea how long she sat there waiting for him to say something. She was aware of him talking, as if he had been talking for some time.

'...and while it would be easy for me to let you go, sure in the knowledge that Markwick would follow you and get him out of Rosalind's way, that wouldn't be really what I wanted, because do you see, in my position, I can still help you – protect you – while you stay in the district, without arousing gossip. You're my patient. But if you leave the district, I can't help you, because to follow you or to arrange for someone else to guard you, would be the one sure way to arouse people's interest and suspicion. I won't have you talked about, Julie.'

She turned to look at him, blinking a little, wondering if she had really heard him say all that, in that special low, fond voice, or whether she had dreamed it.

'Now I want you to promise me you'll stay here, Julie, for a few weeks. That's all. I had it in mind to ask my friend Fisher to investigate Markwick's background, just to see if there was anything at all that we could pin on him, to use to get him off your back. I'm sure there will be something we can use to get at him. But you are not to even hint to him what's going on, or it will spoil everything. Do you understand, Julie?'

He took her chin in his hand, and forced her to look at him.

'I think so,' she said, her voice still thick with sleep. 'But why can't I go to work for your mother's Miss Kemp?'

'Because I want you here, where I can keep an eye on you. You'll be safer here than in some strange place on your own, a long way away from me. Do you understand, Julie?'

'You mean Boyd – he'll follow me.'

She hadn't been following his line of reasoning. She hadn't guessed at the things he had deliberately left unsaid. He sighed. He was playing with fire, he knew, but he wanted, that night, to let her know that she was special to him, even though he had no right to put it into words.

'Something like that. Will you promise me, Julie?'

She promised readily, because now she couldn't shake the weariness off. She wanted to go home, to bed. The last few days had been too full of shocks and excitement for her peace of mind.

'Right. Now I'll drive you home. I want to look at that leg tomorrow, and Jancy will be there too, so don't think up any wonderful excuses to stay away, will you?'

Again she promised, and after that he drove her home.

During the course of the next day, Julie learned that the Mendellini Collar had found a new place of safety. It was locked in the safe in the office of the Hospital Secretary.

Julie heard it before she went to have her leg examined, and she heard other people talking about it when she left Adam and the eminent surgeon, Mr Jancy. She felt that if many more people discussed it, it would again be fair game for people like Boyd to have a shot at removing it.

She said so, to Joan, the clerk she worked with.

'Not on your life, dear. It's as safe as houses, there, because someone's there all the time.'

'Doesn't Mr Rork ever go home, then?'

'Oh, yes, but there's Night Superintendent's office next door, and a night porter on duty at the end of that corridor, and if anyone tried to get to that room, they'd have to pass both. Don't worry, dear, you're not supposed to know about it, and anyway, you're not at the shop while you're here!' and she pulled a comical face at that brilliant piece of reasoning.

Julie did worry, though. She couldn't stop worrying. It was so strange that that piece of jewellery had been in danger already, after Boyd had expressed an interest in it.

It was when she went back to the shop that afternoon that she heard Neville Stannard was to be allowed out of hospital the following day, but he wouldn't be back at the shop at once.

She was not sure whether she was glad or sorry. Sorry because his absence was a continual reminder of the bad luck that Collar – or herself, perhaps – meant for some people. In an obscure way she felt that she had brought no good to Howe's the Jewellers since she had been there.

She wished she could have seen Mr Howe that day, but again he was busy, this time with his accountant.

With Adam no longer taking her around, and Neville still in hospital, it was another day for Julie to get herself home. She avoided the rush hour buses by walking along looking at the shops, waiting until the business crowds had all gone, and in this way she came to the antique dealer's – the one where she had first met Adam outside the hospital.

He remembered her. 'Ah, so, the little friend of my very good customer Mr Hollidge. Come in, come in, do not stand there in the doorway!' he greeted her.

She went in, smiling. 'Did he ever find that gift for his mother?' she asked, looking all round.

'He never came back for it, but I believe that was because of a certain patient of his, no?' and the old man laughed slyly, and winked.

'It could be because of the trouble I brought him, and kept him so fully occupied,' Julie said shortly, 'or it could be because of his anxiety about his wife,' and she looked steadily back at him.

His smile vanished. 'So you know about her. That was a very shocking business, very shocking.'

'How shocking?' Julie asked guardedly.

'Well, you know, my dear, I agree with his mother – that girl should be sent back to the Home. He can say if he likes – she is cured! – but do I believe that? No, but then have I not seen her, sitting in a pub – well, any pub – and staring so longingly at the bottles – you know? I say to myself, that one will be back in trouble very soon. And I go over to her and say, have some food with old Solly, for old times sake, eh? Solly will not eat alone and he is hungry, I say. And she says, oh, what the hell, all right! I will – if you pay. So, I pay. And she eats and I eat, and we talk a little, and I drink horrible tomato juice to keep her company, and there is one more time gone by when she might just have gone over the edge. But for how long. Who can tell?' and he spread his hands eloquently.

Julie nodded, but Solly rushed on to another subject before she could speak.

'Now you, my dear, what about the man old Solly chase away for you that time? He came back, perhaps?'

'Yes, he came back,' she sighed. 'And he's in my life again, and I wish I were a thousand miles away. Now don't you say it's wrong to run away! That may be, but it's still bliss to think of being on the other side of the world, where he can't reach me.'

'I know. Don't I know? A voice inside says run, run – but if you run, it is to a strange place, and there are all these people around you, strangers, and they look at you and they don't know you and they don't care, and you think to yourself, what would I give to have some of those new friends by me to talk to, those new friends I made in the last place? Now, you just tell me – count, count, count on the fingers of your hand – how many new people do you know since you come to Fleckbury? There is old Solly–' and he touched his chest, and then struck off one finger.

Laughing, Julie played the game he had set her. 'Mr Howe himself (oh, yes, I met him in hospital) and his nephew, Mr Gooch and Mr Wexibole, Charlie Carr (I don't like him) and the other man in the shop; my landlady and her husband.'

'And our good friend Mr Hollidge,' Solly put in.

'And his mother–'

'And you know his poor wife?'

'Oh, yes, Rosalind Osborne, but she wouldn't lift a finger to help me.'

'You don't know! You don't know who would help anyone, till the time comes and they do!' he told her fiercely. 'Who else do you know?'

'Oh, hosts of people at the hospital– Peter Lawrence, one of the housemen, and Bert, the ambulance driver, and all the clerks I work with, and two or three ward sisters and–Where's all this getting you?' she broke off to ask him with a sad smile. 'Who of all those would care if I went away?'

'More than you know,' he said. 'I tell you something that will surprise you. There is a woman – in the delicatessen down the street – she does not speak English so good. And she wants a present for her daughter's twenty-first birthday. She hasn't got much money. I say to her, go to Howe's, they are old-established jewellers. She says to me, What, me go to that snooty place? They would throw me out!' He worked those eloquent podgy hands of his to mark the point. 'But she takes my advice. She goes. And she comes back to me with a little brooch – very nice, diamond chips. And she tells me there is a girl there. She was so kind. She has a little limp, she says, but the kindest face, she says. I could look at her smile all the time, she tells me. She didn't make me feel I was just an old woman from the delicatessen, but she makes me feel like an important customer. You know? That is you, *you*, she is talking about! And you say these people will not remember you!'

He persuaded Julie to stay for a cup of coffee with him, and he found a crusty long French loaf with seeds on the top, and cut hunks of it for them both, and put a slice of liver sausage on the top and they sat eating and drinking until the streets were quiet.

'Thank you, but I must go now,' Julie said. 'You've been so kind. I shall remember you.'

'Do better than that,' he said. 'Stay around. Here is where your friends are. Do not run away.'

She walked along to the bus stop, thinking about what he said. He had left her with a warm glowing feeling inside her. But at the bus stop, well, within sight of the shop (and keeping the shop door in sight, no doubt) Boyd lounged against the post.

'I just wondered how much longer you were going to be in there!' he said grimly.

CHAPTER TWELVE

He hadn't got the shiny new car today. It was the old one again, and he was in no mood to make explanations.

'Don't drive me anywhere, Boyd. I'm tired. I want to go home.'

'Rest while I talk to you then,' he said, and drove out of Fleckbury in the direction of Watchford. There was a road going high above the valley. One side of it was a sheer drop, with Fleckbury low down like a lot of toy houses among the trees, the river a pale blue band threading its way in and out of sight. Beyond them was the sugar-loaf hill – St Agnes – and on the other side Watchford, a grey town of factories and half the accidents that filled the Eltonstock casualty wards, because their own hospital couldn't cope.

'This will be a good enough place to pull up and talk,' Boyd said, selecting a rough, stony lay-by. 'Now, I suppose you have heard that the Collar was returned?'

She nodded fearfully. 'So you did have something to do with it! I was afraid you had. But how, how?'

He sat laughing so softly that she could hardly hear him, but his whole frame shook. 'Little Julie, stewing with anxiety, not letting herself be admiring, though she wants to be. Oh, I have to admit that luck went our way. It wasn't quite as we had plotted. Even I couldn't fake an accident like that. No, it was so simple, old Wyndham wouldn't really believe me.'

'Wyndham is a thief too?' Julie whispered.

Boyd looked angry for a moment, then he laughed again. 'Julie, Julie, we are none of us thieves. We have just borrowed the damned thing and now we want to put it back. And for our trouble in getting it out on loan all nice and quiet, Wyndham and I have made a nice little sum.'

'It's thieving,' she said furiously. 'Anyway, how could those children have got hold of it, if someone was borrowing it?'

'Really, I believe you're as dim as you want me to believe! Listen, duckie, no children, no one playing with it – just a clever story for the coppers, otherwise if some grubby kid hadn't handed it in to the police station, what copper would have gone with it like a good boy, to the hospital and the rightful owner? Use your loaf, Julie!'

'Oh, Boyd, Boyd, what am I going to do with you?'

'Ah, now I'm coming to that,' he said, smiling again. 'But first, the set-up. Dian thought it was all a joke and obligingly telephoned the store, then she got cold feet and backed out, so Wyndham promised to telephone and say it was all right. She nearly wrecked the whole scheme when she heard that that fool Stannard had crashed his car and lost the thing. However, the whole point was, our man (road-sweeper to you, dear) was to hold up the traffic and make a jam, and one of us was going to put his arm in and take the case out while everyone was watching the fun, only some silly ass of a learner comes along and nearly messes everything up. However, all's well that ends well. We are but a bunch of amateurs but we have our patches of luck, and this was it. The learner made a real crash (I'm sorry for poor Stannard, of course, but he wasn't hurt, only shaken up, and he can afford to get a new car, and he'll get the insurance anyway) and I have no guarantee that our original plan would have worked, whereas this did.'

'How can you be sure Neville Stannard wasn't hurt? He might have been killed!' Julie stormed.

'You carrying a torch for him, love? I thought it was the old sawbones you were lovesick over.'

'Boyd, I hate you! I shall go and tell everyone—'

'No, dear. No, you won't. Listen, I know
Stannard wasn't hurt, because I was the
helpful chap carrying the brief-case, who
poked his head in the car and tried to help,
only to get hauled out by the ambulance
johnnies and the police – but not before I'd
popped the case of gems in my open brief-
case, eh? Smart, that!'

'I *will* tell everyone—' she said again.

'I wonder if you will, when I've finished
what I have to say to you, love? You see, I
galloped back to our pal who was going to
make the copy. Worked all night on it, with
his two sons, and a thumping good job they
made of it. We were going to get the original
back next day and kid the old baroness that
it was the original we were lending her, then
if anything was said, who cares about a paste
copy?'

'Boyd, I don't believe a word of this rig-
marole. Are you telling me this baroness
doesn't know the real thing from paste?'

'The old dear's eyesight's awfully bad and
she's too vain to admit it. Anyway, she
carried it off all right.'

'When?'

'Last night. The Ball was actually mentioned in the papers, and there were photo-
graphs – not of her. No one would want to
photograph that old hag.'

'But didn't anyone recognise the Mendellini Collar?' Julie gasped.

'Is it supposed to be world-famous, then?' he asked innocently. 'I thought it was a local monstrosity made by a local jeweller for some ghastly trade type from New York who was loaded with cash and no savvy or taste. No? Well, be that as it may, some fool of a secretary put the idea around that the Collar was a family heirloom smuggled out of Hungary or somewhere, and that was what was mentioned in the papers. So – you see my difficulty, love? We have the original on our hands, returned by a grateful near-sighted baroness with cash for our services, and we have to put it back where it ought to be before the owners catch on that they are guarding the paste copy.'

'Oh, no, Boyd. No!' Julie whispered. 'How will you do it?'

'Not me, love – *you*.'

It took her some seconds to take that in. Boyd said quickly, 'Now, now Julie – before you explode, there's one thing you ought to know, and I somehow think it may persuade you to change your tune.' He smiled. 'There's a chap who's under the impression that an awful blunder's been made by the authorities, over old Reuben Floy's inquest. He is prepared to come forward and say that it was no accident, that you, in fact, ran the poor old boy down while incapable of driving straight. He is prepared to say he'd taken you to a party and you'd had a couple too many, and he'd jumped from the car to save his own life.'

Her eyes were wide with horror. 'Where has this witness been all this time?'

'He's one of those toughs who knock about the globe scratching a living. He's only just back from someone or other's private scrap in Africa – can't think which side he was on – and now he's back and looking up old newspapers, he's just catching up on things. Rum type, but d'you see, love, if you help me out over getting the perishing Collar back intact, I might just persuade this enthusiastic type that he's suffering from a touch of the sun, and send him back to where he came from without telling a soul what he thinks, and then you'd be safe. See what I mean?'

'No. I don't. It sounds as if you've got someone who'll tell a lot of lies about me if I don't do what you want, but there's a horrid name for that.'

'You listen to me, love. You don't *know* what happened for sure that day – you've said so often enough. But I tell you this – no one believed the garbled story you told 'em in hospital about you racing around streets getting some chap away from some others in a car. They thought you were light-headed. You don't even know the result of the inquest, do you? Too scared to go to a newspaper office and read it up for yourself, weren't you – and why? You tell me!'

'But I wasn't at any party, Boyd. They would have given me an alcohol test–'

'You were trapped in that car too long, Julie, for a test to be any use. Just you be a sensible girl and do this one thing for me and then you clear off nice and quietly somewhere and it'll all blow over. No one will know it's you. Now listen.'

She sat frozen, while his voice flowed over her.

'You take the case in your arms, between some files from your office, and you go up to the Hospital Secretary, in broad daylight and bang on his door.'

'But why? I don't have to go up to him!'

'You will say you've come to ask him to put a patient's diamond rings in the safe while she goes for her operation. What more natural? (They will be fetched from the patient by someone, who will give them to you, don't worry.) Then the other person will create a racket outside the door (after giving him time to open the safe) and while he runs out to see what's going on, you switch your lot of jewels for those in the case in the safe. When he comes back (having found the cry of Fire! was a false alarm) you will be standing innocently holding the rings to be put away. Got it?'

'It won't work,' Julie moaned.

'It will – it will have to! – or we shall all be in queer street, because, love, it has worked out rather too fine in time for even my liking. Now, let's go over it again.'

'How can you prove that this man is telling the truth about me? I don't think anyone will believe him.'

'Oh, yes, they will,' Boyd said grimly. 'I personally shall see to that. Now, will you listen to me and go over the details again?'

She nodded, but in her heart she was thinking, 'I won't. I'll take the originals to Mr Howe and tell him the truth. I'll stop Boyd once and for all.'

Something of this must have shown in her face for Boyd said, very softly, 'If you've any idea of taking the stuff to the police or old Howe, you'll be left holding the can, baby, I absolutely promise you. I can run, you can't.'

'But how do I know that this isn't another paste copy? How was it so many people were in it? Boyd, I don't believe–'

'You just do it, love, or you'll find that somehow the police will receive an anonymous telephone call saying you have got the Collar and that you took it. You remember that – I'll hang it on you somehow if you won't do just this little thing for me.'

Boyd left it at that and drove her home.

Gideon was talking to his neighbour over the back fence. Vera was out, but had left Julie's dinner in the oven. A note propped on the kitchen table said so.

The dinner was dry round the edges, and barely warm. Julie ate half of it at the kitchen table, then left the rest, because it was choking her.

Gideon was still talking. She hesitated to interrupt him, so she walked the streets, thinking.

Thinking over all Gideon had said to her that night by the river; a conversation that had presented everything in his own simple sane light of reasoning, and which she knew wouldn't work out in her own special circumstances. Thinking over all that Adam had said to her that evening, and all that his mother had planned for her with that Miss Kemp, so many miles away from Fleckbury and Boyd; thinking, moreover, of what it would all be like here, if she did what Boyd had asked her to, and then quietly slipped away.

What would all her friends think of her? It was unlikely that she would get out of this without speculation and suspicion. It was always the same, when she was persuaded to help Boyd; he got away with it, every time.

She must have walked for close on two hours, before she came to any decision. Long before then she had thought of several different plans, only to discard them all. She knew a lot about precious stones, learned from Reuben Floy, and if only she could get

211

hold of a jeweller's glass to put in her eye and inspect the Collar now reposing in the safe in the Hospital Secretary's room, it would solve all her problems. She was reasonably certain that she would be able to tell if it were the real stones or fakes.

Until then, a dozen problems beset her. It was incredible to Julie that neither police nor the hospital authorities would check first to see if those were the real stones, but of course, they didn't know that a copy was being made. And now Julie was asking herself, was it a copy in that safe, or the real thing. If it were the real thing, and she was being given a paste copy to put in its place, under cover of Boyd's plausible story of replacing the real thing, what was the position then? Boyd and his accomplice would make off with the real Collar, and Julie would be suspected of stealing it, since she would be the one who had been left in the room with the safe open.

The more she thought of it, the more she thought this probable, for she only had Boyd's word for it that an impoverished baroness was paying for the loan of the necklace for a special occasion; only Boyd's word that such a person existed. Of course, Julie could look it up in the newspaper files, if there were time, but there wasn't. She supposed she could telephone some London newspaper to ask if such a ball had taken place, but Boyd had been careful to omit to tell her which it had been, and where it had been held – if, indeed it had.

The question of time pressing, nagged at her. There was only between now and tomorrow morning at eleven, to do anything, and what could she do? Tell Gideon about it? She knew from the first what his advice would be: go to the police. Gideon had an unfailing faith in the power of his local police station. Julie thought about it, and saw herself giving a lot of personal details which would sound like nothing else but a garbled story. If they believed her, she might well be in trouble herself, but if they didn't she would have wasted a lot of time to no good purpose.

No, telling Gideon wasn't the way, and in any case, he would be one more person to know about it. The fewer to know about this, the better.

Who, then, could she go to for advice? Neville Stannard? Oh, no, he was too close to the whole thing, and for the same reason old Cedric Howe was not the person to confide in. Old Solly? But his advice, she was sure, would run parallel with Gideon's.

That only left one thing to do: if she didn't want to consult Adam himself, then she must resort to letting things ride, calling Boyd's bluff, inviting him to do his worst.

Everything in her recoiled from such a

course, because she just didn't remember enough about that accident to be sure if she herself had been responsible for Reuben Floy's death. The only thing she could be sure of was that she hadn't been to a party and hadn't been drinking, but that wouldn't help her if Boyd were to be believed. If only she knew what the real result of Reuben Floy's inquest had been!

No, she must telephone Adam, ask to talk to him, tell him about this latest development and abide by what he suggested.

She called his mother's home from a box near No. 16. Without realising it, she had almost wandered back to her lodgings, but sleep was a long way off now. She had to get this clear in her mind before she went to bed tonight.

Mrs Hollidge answered the telephone and when Julie told her who was calling, dismay was in the woman's voice.

'What do you want my son for?' she asked sharply.

'Something has happened, and I need his advice very badly,' Julie said.

'Now look, my dear, he has enough worries, what with his unfortunate marriage, and something that has happened and he has been called back to the hospital tonight. He won't be in until very late indeed, and I won't have him bothered then.'

'No. I see,' Julie said.

Something in her voice worried the older woman. 'Can't you confide in me?' she asked Julie.

'No. No, it doesn't matter. It was something I had to do and I didn't want to and I was going to be guided by him, but it doesn't matter,' she said again. 'I'll do it. I expect it will be the quickest way out in the end.'

'Well, it all sounds very mysterious, but when is it to happen?' Adam's mother asked, faint amusement in her voice.

'Tomorrow,' Julie said. 'And then I'm going away. Quickly, so that no one knows where I am. I owe it to myself to get away like that. I'm so tired of everything.'

'Then why don't you let me make all the arrangements to take the job I was telling you about?' Mrs Hollidge asked. 'I assure you, Julie, whatever you think you heard my son say about it, it isn't like that. I wouldn't send you to a place where you would get exhausted running about. It's a good home, a comfortable lodging and your friends would never find you. Now what do you say?'

'All right,' Julie said. She was giving in to Boyd, so why not to Mrs Hollidge too?

Mrs Hollidge was so pleased at Julie's capitulation that she didn't stop to listen to the timbres in Julie's voice: despair, extreme fatigue, the air of giving in to anything at any price. All Mrs Hollidge could think of

215

was that she was getting this girl away, as far as possible, out of Adam's reach, and soon she would have Rosalind back in that Home, and then her beloved son would be able to leave Eltonstock behind and look to the dizzy heights of Harley Street.

'Now listen carefully, dear. I want you to get packed tonight, and I'll have a car over for you at eleven tomorrow.'

'I can't get back to my lodgings from the hospital by then, Mrs Hollidge.'

'Then don't go to the hospital, silly girl!'

'I must,' Julie said flatly and was going to ring off, but Mrs Hollidge said hastily,

'All right, I'll have a car at the gates of the hospital. In fact, dear, I'll see you off at the Junction. We can pick up the train to Carlisle there. It will make an easier journey for you.'

Julie kept saying 'all right' to everything she said, so that in the end Mrs Hollidge wondered whether she was really taking it all in. So she made Julie repeat it, just to make sure.

'Now do be ready, dear, and I'm sure you won't regret taking this step. And Julie, please don't try to contact my son. Let's not worry him with this until you are quite settled at Miss Kemp's. Then I'm sure you'll find it so peaceful that you won't want to hear of Eltonstock and Fleckbury again.'

'No,' Julie agreed, and remembered at last

to say thank you for what Mrs Hollidge was doing on her behalf.

Gideon had come in by the time Julie arrived back at the house. She just had time to tell him that she was leaving the next day for a job somewhere, when Vera arrived.

'But you can't leave all of a sudden like this!' Vera exploded, her brows knit in a tight frown. She hated to have her plans put out of gear, and she had planned to make Julie comfortable for a long time. The letting of that room was sometimes a chancy thing; Julie had been a quiet, likeable lodger.

Gideon cut in. 'She's had a rare fine offer of a live-in job, and you'd be the first, I know, dear, to advise Julie to grab any such chance. You know you're always saying take what comes and don't consider anyone else but yourself.'

It was so rare that Gideon did such a thing that Vera was for a moment without words. Julie hastily explained: 'It's a job with a rich old lady – I've been recommended by some- one who knows her personally, otherwise I would never have known about the job. I don't feel I shall ever have such a chance again. I shall hate leaving here but I have to think of every angle.'

After they had discussed her arrangements for packing and the journey and accepted the fact that she didn't want to disclose her destination in case her cousin came to look her up before she had settled in, they let her go to bed. Vera might swallow that reason but Gideon knew better. His sad look reproached Julie for running away from Boyd, after all he himself had said to Julie against running away.

CHAPTER THIRTEEN

As Julie was the latest recruit to the Appointments Office, hers was the job to do the occasional message, so there was nothing strange about her having to take files up to the third floor, and a patient's few valuables to the Hospital Secretary.

Until the moment Boyd had arranged for the switch of the Collar to happen, Julie hadn't given it a thought as to who his accomplice in the hospital would be. Try as she would, she couldn't rid her mind of that word 'accomplice' and she thought, as she waited in the corridor near the Women's Medical Ward, that it would be one of the orderlies that Boyd had charmed. But the only person in sight at the appointed time was Rosalind Osborne, pushing her trolley of books.

'Hello, chum,' she greeted Julie. 'Here we are. Your pal Boyd says you know what to do with them,' and she handed Julie the two rings.

Julie stared at her in horror. 'You?' she whispered.

'Now who did you think it would be – Matron?' Rosalind said, with her throaty chuckle.

'Oh, do keep your voice down. It's supposed to be all very hush-hush,' Julie pleaded.

'Honey, if I'm to help, I do it in my own way,' Adam's wife said, and there was a glint in her eyes.

'But why? I mean, you hardly know Boyd!'

'Now you watch it, chum. He may be your cousin, but he's a friend of mine, seeing as he remembers seeing me in show business. Now anyone who remembers me in that dazzling few years of my young life is very dear to my heart. Besides, I just like Boyd, and that's it! So don't you say anything against him.' She grinned. 'Take this, too. You'll want it.'

'All right,' Julie said, in surprise and went on up to the Hospital Secretary's room.

What was Boyd thinking of, entrusting this job to that irresponsible person, Rosalind Osborne? Fancy giving her the rings, and finally the files and the case of jewels, casually like that, in an open corridor! Oh, well, perhaps the mere casualness of the move had been disarming, and no one would have thought another word about it if they had seen.

Mr Rork was on the telephone, and signalled Julie to wait a minute. She stood clutching her things to her. If he saw that it was only a couple of rings, he might be tempted to come off the telephone for a minute, and take them from her and that would ruin the whole plan.

Julie stood there sweating with fear about Rosalind. Surely she wasn't the person detailed to shout 'Fire'? Would she get there at the right time? Supposing she called out too soon? They hadn't allowed for the Secretary being on the telephone!

Suddenly he put the phone down and smiled at her. 'Well, what have you got for me?' and he made to take the files.

'No, these aren't for you, Mr Rork. It's the patient's rings,' Julie said, and gave them to him.

'Oh, yes. Which patient entrusted these to me?'

Julie gaped at him. She had forgotten to ask, in her surprise at seeing Rosalind give them to her. And Rosalind had forgotten to tell her.

'I'm sorry, I can't remember,' Julie said. 'In Women's Medical, anyway.'

'I think I've seen Mrs Dean wearing these. Short and fat, was she, with greying hair and a lot of make-up? Jolly person?'

It seemed fairly safe to say yes, so Julie nodded amiably and was relieved to see him turn to the safe, with his keys. And then the whole plan collapsed.

'I won't put them in the wall safe, as we have something rather special and important there,' Mr Rork said pleasantly. 'I'll just put them for safety in this small safe. They'll be quite all right here, and I expect the patient will be shouting for them back as soon as she comes to. They always want them after coming down from theatre and finding they're still with us. Bucks them up.'

Julie nearly died of dismay. Now what was she to do? Hadn't Boyd known there were two places of safety? Hadn't he anticipated this?

She could only say yes, and thank him and get ready to back out of the room. It was at that moment that the commotion started in the corridor outside. Someone staggered and fell heavily. Mr Rork stood poised at the small safe, then slammed it shut before he hurried out to see what was wrong. As he opened the door, Julie caught sight of Rosalind, cheerfully but ineffectually trying to raise herself from the ground.

As Mr Rork stopped dead at the sight of her, she raised a hand in greeting. 'Hello, Rorky, chum! How are you?' she shouted, her voice slurred, and a silly grin on her face. And for good measure, she started to sing an uncertain line from the old music-hall song about the unfortunate girl who was only a bird in a gilded cage.

Mr Rork was horrified. 'Mrs Hollidge– Good heavens, this is terrible! Here – what's-your-name! – Miss Quinn,' he called, remembering Julie's name with a magnificent feat of memory since he hardly had anything to do with her, 'Help me get Mrs Hollidge up, while I send down for her husband. No, wait, better not advertise it by using the telephone – I'll go down and find him personally, if I can. Here, get her into my room.'

'I want the Ladies',' Rosalind said loudly and firmly.

'Don't worry, you go down for Mr Hollidge. I'll look after her,' Julie said.

Rosalind leaned heavily on Julie. Julie was horrified to detect a faint odour of whisky. No wonder poor Mr Rork had rushed like that. But Rosalind had been all right downstairs! Julie looked anxiously at her.

'You are not supposed to be out here,' Rosalind said, straightening up. 'You are supposed to be in there making the switch.'

'You *have* been drinking!' Julie gasped.

'Just enough to make it auth-authentic,' Rosalind said, giggling. 'Old Rorky wouldn't have gone down so quick if I hadn't. Now come on – I haven't got all day.'

The plan had collapsed. What would happen if Rosalind in this half truculent mood, got a look in that room and saw that neither of the safes were open?

Mr Rork was coming back. Julie felt herself driven to do something. She wasn't sure what Boyd was up to or whether indeed this was the paste set she had, but if she wasn't careful she herself would be held up and lose that train that promised freedom, from Boyd, from all her troubles. Run, her mind said.

So she thrust the files and what was hidden between them, at Rosalind. 'Your timing was wrong. I've done it. Here, take them. You'd better use the stairs at the end. I'm coming, too.'

Rosalind needed no second telling. She could hear Adam's voice. It echoed down the long corridor connecting this one. She shot down the stairs. That was the last Julie saw of her.

She waited inside the Night Superintendent's room until Mr Rork and Adam had satisfied themselves that neither of the girls were in the room, but presumably in the Ladies' Room in the next corridor. They went charging out and buttonholed a nurse to go and search there, while Julie followed at a distance, limping along at her own pace till she reached the lift. She didn't return to the office.

Quietly she took off her overall and put on her outdoor things, and went out. Mrs

Hollidge was waiting for her. They went back to Fleckbury and collected Julie's luggage and said good-bye to the Leighs.

This was the aftermath. Julie's heart was hammering and she had been shaking all over since they had left Eltonstock.

'Are you all right, my dear?' Mrs Hollidge asked, taking her eyes off the road for a quick peep at Julie's white face.

'Yes. It's just ... another upheaval. I'd like to be settled. Peace. No worries.'

'Oh, you will, you will, I assure you!' Mrs Hollidge enthused, washed with relief that Julie wasn't going to say she felt too ill to go after all. 'Now I want to tell you about Miss Kemp and her house and the village and all the things you should know about her. Oh, and about the jeweller's where you work – if there's anything to be tidied up there, you'd better tell me now. I'll see to it for you.'

Julie felt an insane desire to laugh at the top of her voice and say, oh, there is, there's the little matter of the Mendellini Collar – it was stolen and I've just given it to your daughter-in-law and she's been drinking!

Julie caught her breath. The thought had brought another in its train: *if* that had been the real one she was supposed to have put back, then she had given it to Boyd. Made him a present of it!

But supposing ... supposing it had only been the paste one, and he had lied to her, and cheated her into being prepared to unknowingly take the real one out of the safe and put the paste one back? In that case, he had been planning to go away with the real one, break it up, and share it out among those concerned. Why hadn't she thought of it before? Of course that must be it – there were too many of them in it to be satisfied with the fee that the impoverished baroness was supposed to have paid for the loan of the Collar.

Julie was so hot by the time Mrs Hollidge – still talking brightly and encouragingly – drove into the yard of Eltonstock Halt and parked the car, that she as sure her companion would notice. Following in the trail of that thought, it would appear that Julie had sent the paste copy back to Boyd, in Rosalind's hands. And what would Boyd, in his fury, do to Julie when he discovered what she had done? He would never believe that it hadn't been by design, but because his clever plan had gone wrong. Boyd's plans usually went wrong because they were so fantastic, too much depending on luck, and as he had sardonically said, he was but an amateur.

Mrs Hollidge was altogether different in her manner today. She liked Julie as a person, and the fact that now Julie was going out of her son's life, led Mrs Hollidge to feel that she could afford to show her liking.

She bought Julie a generous supply of

glossy magazines, a lunch pack, a box of chocolates and a personal present from herself in an envelope to be opened on the journey.

'You don't have to do all this,' Julie said quietly. 'You've been more than good to me, finding me a resident job and bringing me to the station. I'm grateful.'

'Oh, my dear, don't give me gratitude,' Mrs Hollidge said, flushing. 'In other circumstances I would have been only too happy to have you in our family circle as a friend, but you do understand how difficult it all is, don't you?'

'Perhaps I understand better than you do,' Julie told her, bleakly, and as the train started to move, there was mercifully no time for Mrs Hollidge to ask for an explanation.

Julie sat watching the telephone poles flash by, with a feeling that she had been drained of all emotion. She had been plucked bodily from the place she had tried to carve out for herself, like a small field animal toed by an unfriendly boot out of its nest. She was going into the unknown again, and this time it was not of her own choosing.

And her heart ached for Adam. Now she was actually on the train and the miles were piling up between them, it dawned on her that she would never see him again and it was more than she could bear. For such a little while he had been in her life almost every day, and his leaving had made such a huge gap. It hadn't been so bad while she had been working in the hospital; there was a chance of seeing him, and there were those examinations on her leg. He was there, near at hand, and the unspoken thought was there, too, that if she needed him she had only to call on him.

Now that had gone. His mother had seen to that. His mother and the force of circumstances had worked together, and now she was alone, with only her memories of him. Bitter-sweet memories like the night when she had almost fallen into the river and he had put out a hand to grasp her and held her to him as if he would never let her go. And memories of those two occasions when it seemed that he would inevitably take her into his arms and kiss her, and then by a superhuman effort he had refrained.

Well, of course he couldn't, she scolded herself; he was already married and a man like Adam, with a career such as his, didn't play fast and loose with some other girl. And she herself wouldn't have wanted it. Then why, her heart cried, why do two people have to care for each other when they have no right to?

She forced herself to look at the glossy magazines and to eat the lunch pack much too soon. The journey seemed interminable. Feeling hungry again, she took the second lunch on the train, dipping into her small store of money, for the sake of something to do.

The train journey ended at Carlisle, and then there was a hired car to meet her and to take her and her luggage through unfamiliar streets and lanes in the darkness, the rain and the wind. An unfriendly night to start a new job in a strange place.

Too late she remembered one aspect of her swift going away from Fleckbury; it might have been a smart move to evade Boyd and his friends, but it was a questionable thing to do from the point of view of those friends she herself had made. Those at the hospital, and the people in the shop, would naturally wonder what was behind such a sudden departure, however well Mrs Hollidge went about the task she had undertaken to tidy up loose ends and make explanations. They would still wonder, and probably suspect that something was wrong, even if everything were tidied up.

But what else could she have done, without disclosing her destination? In saying goodbye to people, it wasn't possible to keep her destination a secret, without further suspicions. The Leighs, for a start, had thought it very odd.

The hired car seemed to be making quite a journey. Julie wondered about the expense, but later she was to find that Miss Kemp had no car of her own, and didn't employ anyone who could drive or look after one even if she desired one. It was her habit to order everything by telephone, and when a piece of personal shopping was necessary, she hired a car, and never from the same firm. She had a horror of people becoming familiar. In the days that followed, the eccentric old woman often told Julie that the only way to extract service from people nowadays was to keep hiring new ones. Strangers were careful, because they wanted the business; once let them get to know you, and used to you, and they forgot their manners.

She was a small woman, Julie discovered. Small and indeterminate of age, anywhere between the fifties and sixties; plain in features, mousy in colouring, but a very determined little woman, of fixed ideas.

Julie didn't see her that night. She was conscious of the hired car going into what seemed a dark tunnel. Next day, in broad daylight, Julie found this to be an over-grown unkempt drive, long and moss-covered, through disuse. Rank undergrowth replaced the once tidy bushes that flanked it; tall trees almost met overhead. And at the end of it, the house stood; a flat-faced, darkish house, with blank eyes of windows, some shuttered, others kept covered by thick lace curtains. Not an inspiring house in which to live.

Inside, the lights seemed rather low-powered. Later, she was to recognise this as one of Miss Kemp's economy measures, though Miss Kemp wasn't hard up. There was a lot of dark furnishings, a lot of Victorian pieces of furniture, good but dull. The place was adequately clean but by no means gleaming with polish. This was later explained by the fact that Miss Kemp kept only the one servant, a hard worker named Harriet, who had been with her all her life: but the house was big for one person to keep clean.

Harriet was a big, strong woman, said locally to be not very bright. She showed Julie her room, a rather bare room at the end of the first floor corridor, and at once Julie saw that the conditions hadn't changed for the last sixty years. There was even a jug and basin on the marble-topped wash-stand. But there was a room that had been converted to a rather primitive bathroom, next door.

Her room, Julie found, did have a writing table, and there was a big book-case, and plenty of cupboard space. Harriet stood looking at Julie's two cases – all her worldly possessions – and it was the one time in the six months that Julie stayed there, that Harriet showed the slightest curiosity.

'I bet you got pretty things,' Harriet said.

'No, not really. Would you like to see what I have got?' Julie asked, feeling sorry for the plainness of Harriet's clothes, and the absence of make-up on the big dough-like face.

Harriet hesitated, then said, 'No, there's the washing-up to be done.'

'Shall I help you?' Julie asked, not quite sure what her duties would be.

'You can come down and get your own supper,' Harriet offered. 'The madam won't see you tonight.'

So Julie followed her down the interminable passages to a big bare stone-floored kitchen, as primitive as the rest of the house.

The following day Julie met Miss Kemp, and after the first long, preliminary stare, Miss Kempt said, 'I have sound judgement. I think you will do.'

'But you don't know anything about me. You haven't any references. I did rather wonder about you taking me into your employ, but Mrs Hollidge said you'd leave it to her to find someone. I hope it will be all right,' Julie said doubtfully. She was finding the house and its contents and these two women, rather overpowering.

'Mrs Hollidge I don't know very well. She is a friend of a friend of mine,' Miss Kemp said firmly. 'But I understand that you have been either in (or on the verge of) some sort of trouble, and that you are ready to take anything, so long as it is a roof over your head. That is good enough for me.'

Julie felt a sense of betrayal. Yet perhaps Mrs Hollidge hadn't meant it like that. She had probably felt it was the best and only thing for Julie. After all, to be connected with Boyd and the odd things he did, was no recommendation, either for a job or to be closely connected with a member of the Hollidge family, when looked at from Adam's mother's viewpoint, Julie decided, trying desperately to be fair.

'You will ask Harriet to show you over the house and grounds, and when I am dressed, we will begin our day's work,' Miss Kemp said. 'I expect you to be willing, neat and tidy, and contented. More than that I do not ask.'

That, of course, was an understatement. In the days that followed, Julie found that Miss Kemp's method was to start a working day with questioning Julie about herself for ten minutes, and then to dismiss her to that impersonal realm where Julie's function was just to take letters and perform those duties that she had been engaged for: to walk the dog (an old disagreeable beast) and to take her own daily dose of exercise and fresh air; to dust the hundreds of small ornaments, books and pieces of furniture that Harriet hadn't time for, and to read aloud dull books that sent her to sleep.

It was a strange house, a long way from the nearest village, hemmed in by low hills. There was no radio or television, no newspapers or magazines. Miss Kemp had no interest in such things, and Harriet apparently could neither read nor write, and in any case, she had no time. When she wasn't scrubbing or doing the washing, she was cooking, bottling, or making bread. There were times when Julie found her precariously climbing the rickety steps to get up to the high ceilings, a rag round her sparse hair, a long cobweb-broom in her bony hands. Her whole life seemed bent on doing her chores, and when she went to bed she slept like the dead.

The muffling effect of Harriet's dull features and manner, and Miss Kemp's preoccupation with her missionary contacts overseas, made Julie feel, at the end of the first week, that she had made a mistake of mistakes.

She had one afternoon off per week, but as it didn't happen to coincide with the times of buses or trains into Carlisle, that left only the village to go into. Julie had to set her teeth at the thought of staying there in that house indefinitely.

Miss Kemp took her in the hired car to Carlisle once a month, shopping, but it was dull shopping for house linen, and stuff to make children's clothing for the missionary interests she had. Julie couldn't see how anyone with only herself to please, and quite a lot of money, could contrive to live such a dull, uninformed life as Miss Kemp.

Yet in its way, it had the compensation of offering Julie a bolt-hole. Boyd would surely never find her here.

Every time she thought of writing to the Leighs, she was deterred, by the thought of how Boyd used to hang around their house, and if he found a letter lying around in her writing, he would see the postmark and know the district where she was. That deterrent was sufficient, yet every month, when she was paid, and she wondered what to do with the amount she allotted to herself for spending money, she thought wistfully of stamps, writing letters, getting in touch with the people she had known.

It was a sad temptation not to write to Solly, who wouldn't have any connection with Boyd. But then, Julie thought, Solly might not remember her, in spite of his offer of friendship. She was, after all, just a girl who had come into the shop with Adam, and it might look as if she were trying to get news of Adam, through Solly. As she *was,* she caught herself up quickly. The aching yearning to hear about Adam grew with each month.

Sometimes she wondered if she dare write to Mrs Hollidge, but Adam's mother had made it clear that she didn't want the acquaintance to be kept up.

Julie had to remind herself that if Adam wanted to know how she was, he knew where she had gone, and he had only to write – as her one-time doctor – to ask about her leg, and which hospital she was attending. So she told herself, but a voice in her head would sharply remind her that he wouldn't be likely to do that. His mother would have told him that Julie knew of the hospital in Carlisle, but that she had decided not to attend anywhere again for that leg of hers.

Julie had been with Miss Kemp for six months when the day came that gave her a measure of freedom that went to her head. Miss Kemp gave her a shopping list and said she was to go by herself in the hired car that day, because she had a visitor coming.

Harriet said sourly to Julie in the kitchen, 'It's that lawyer chap. Comes once a year. She changes her Will. Don't ask me why. Running up and down stairs with trays of tea and coffee, making more work for a body.'

Julie didn't care. She was thrilled, for the first time in a deadly six months stay in that house. For the very first time she would be going to the shops by herself.

The hire car man was a young one today. He looked at Julie's shining young face and said, 'I've got some business I want to attend to. I've been engaged for the afternoon, so you needn't be in a hurry, miss.'

She nodded, and went to the store Miss Kemp favoured, and concentrated on the list in her hand. There might be time to work in a film or something. Just a news cinema would be nice.

In the end she just dawdled round the shops until she came to a local newspaper office.

She sat devouring local and national events of that month, and then back and back through the months since she had come here. She felt like a traveller in the desert, returning to civilisation.

In her heart, all she really wanted to see was news of what had happened in Fleckbury six months ago, and whether there was any mention of the theft of a piece of jewellery called the Mendellini Collar, but if there had been, these newspapers hadn't heard of it.

She sighed, and got up to go out. She had been there an hour. She would have to go without her tea if she wanted to be back in time.

But the taste of civilisation had got into her and now she wanted to hear from her friends. A mood of madness took her and she decided to telephone Fleckbury – the neighbour with the phone in his house – and speak to Gideon. Once the idea took root, she couldn't shift it. She went to the car park and found the hire car, and asked the driver to take her shopping parcels from her, and to wait a little longer while she made a telephone call.

He grinned and winked at her and told her to take her time. He was sitting comfortably reading a racing paper, a cigarette drooping from his lips.

Julie hurried back to the nearest Post Office and got change before she went into the booth. Today, because she was excited and happy, her leg wasn't troubling her so much.

Now, now she would hear from someone who knew her! She stilled the nagging voice inside her which would keep asking her if her one-time landlord would even remember her name, and finally got the number. Gideon must have been in the man's garden, for he came in at once to the telephone.

'*Who* is it?' Plainly he couldn't believe it was Julie.

She told him, twice to make sure, and that it was a long-distance call and that she had been in a town for once, and thought she would like to know if he and Vera were all right.

'Yes, but what about you, lass? We made sure you'd come back at once after what happened. Have you been ill, then? Or maybe abroad?'

'No, I've been here all the time. Why, what did happen?' She caught at her throat, and into her mind shot the thought: something's happened to Adam. But of course that was absurd – who would expect her to hurry back, for someone who should have been no more than her doctor at the hospital?

'It's your cousin Boyd, lass,' Gideon said carefully. 'He had an accident. Didn't you even know about it, then?'

'Boyd?' She whispered the name, and leaned against the wall of the phone booth. 'What happened to him? Where is he?'

'Why, lass, I don't rightly know how to tell you, on this thing, seeing as the pips'll be going soon, but the plain fact is, he was in someone's car and it went over the edge, on that road above us, going to Watchford. You know? Sheer drop, it is. Don't take on, lass, I don't suppose he knew a thing about it. Nor the other one with him.'

'Oh, I didn't know,' she said, her voice a mere thread of sound. 'When did it happen?'

'That's the funny thing about it, lass. It was the day you went away.'

'*Wha-at?*'

The pips went, but she fed more money in. 'Mr Leigh, do you think you could write a long letter and tell me all about it? I feel such a long way away, and I'm working for someone, and I don't think I could get free to come just now.'

'Are you sure you can't come, lass? Not just for a day or two? We'd put you up and gladly,' he said wistfully.

'I'll see,' she said. 'I'll see.'

When she left the telephone box, she was shaking all over. Why hadn't Mrs Hollidge written and told her? Adam must have told his mother why she was so anxious to get away. Adam must surely know where she was!

She went back in the hire car. There was no time for anything else. She would have liked to telephone Solly for his version of it. He must know! She would have liked to telephone the shop to find out if the necklace was safe, but of course, she couldn't do that, even if she had the time. No one must know that she had such an interest in it.

Only by going back and talking to people could she find out all those things.

Suddenly she knew she must go back. Surely Miss Kemp would let her have a couple of days off? Wasn't it called compassionate leave?

She decided to ask the old lady, but for once Miss Kemp was unco-operative.

'I cannot spare you now. If this near relative of yours died so long ago, how was it you only just heard of it? Besides, I understood that you had no one. You don't receive any letters.'

'I would like to go, Miss Kemp. I would like to have your permission to go, but if you won't give it to me, I still have to go. It will be a pity, but I must. Don't you see?' Julie said.

'Then if you go, without my permission, you terminate your employment here. That, too, would be a pity, since I have altered my Will today, and mentioned you in it.'

'That's kind of you, but I can't help it,' Julie said.

In the morning, a letter came from Gideon. He must have gone and written it at once, and made a special journey into Eltonstock to catch the last London collection.

It was brief but shatteringly to the point. 'It was a rum do altogether, lass,' he wrote, after the preliminaries in which he stated he could have been knocked down with a feather to hear her voice on the telephone. 'Your cousin Boyd wasn't driving that car– I never had such a shock in my life as when we heard the news over the wireless – it was that poor wife of Mr Hollidge who was driving it, and there's been rumours that she'd been drinking. Gone back to it after all that time. Shocking business, it was. Mr Hollidge, of course, he didn't stay in the town. Not after that, for what with his mother's illness and being took off – oh, but you won't know about that either, will you? I was forgetting. She got pneumonia. Vera, she said, you'd think those doctors could look after their own mothers better, but it seemed she hadn't been well for a while, and she wasn't over-strong. You never know, do you? Anyway what with his wife, and then his mother, I suppose he felt he didn't want to stay at the Eltonstock General. We miss him. Rum thing about your cousin, though – they found a paste copy of that Mendellini Collar in the wreck of the car. No one could make out how that came to be there.'

His writing became less decipherable as he said he was rushing for the post, but he added a postscript. The Collar had been sold to Dian Ackery's family for the aunt after all, and Dian Ackery had been married to Neville Stannard and the old gentleman was now out of hospital and much better, and Gideon had to leave off there because of going on his bike to Eltonstock to get the London mail.

Julie sat staring at the letter for so long that Harriet started banging about, to remind her that breakfast had to be cleared.

What a lot Gideon had managed to pack into those two pages. Boyd dead, Rosalind dead, Mrs Hollidge dead, and Adam no longer there. There didn't seem much point in leaving here, Julie reflected.

And then, quite suddenly, she realised that she had no reason for staying. She was free! Free to go and find out for herself what the truth of Reuben Floy's death had been from old newspaper files, and if indeed she had been the cause of it. For her own peace of mind, she knew she had to do that, and then ... her life was her own, to please herself.

She smothered the thought that her life wasn't very attractive, stretching ahead in all its barrenness, without Adam, for if he were free too, and he hadn't contacted her, although he knew where she was, it rather pointed to the fact that he had meant it when he had protested friendship only. Perhaps, after six months of freedom, he was already married to someone else, or about to be. Anyway, Gideon hadn't said where Adam had gone.

She told Miss Kemp that she had decided to go, as there were things she had to see to, and she terminated her employment there. Miss Kemp sat staring at her, thwarted by an employee, angrily aware that if she had given Julie time off, the girl would have come back. But being Miss Kemp, she couldn't make the gesture now and climb down. So she let Julie go.

Julie arrived in London with mixed feelings. The last time she had been here, she had been a patient, fresh from being pinned under that car. She shuddered as she remembered it.

Firmly she set about finding a room in a hostel and depositing her luggage. Tomorrow she must find out about Reuben. Tonight she would go around London, renew her acquaintance with the city, try and drive out this sense of returning to her old life with Boyd.

Her leg started to throb, after she had been walking an hour. The Embankment stretched endlessly and the Thames was grey and sluggish. She felt unaccountably depressed, and made her way back towards her hostel.

On the way, she found a Public Library still open, and went inside to sit down. Inevitably she found herself getting off the shelves the thick volume that had been tantalising her, to look up Adam's name and details. There wasn't much she didn't know, except the places where he was educated, but it was a bitter-sweet pleasure reading about him in print. But his present address wasn't there. Well, how could it be, she jeered at herself? How could it be in there, when he had only left the town less than six months ago? Anyway, he might have gone straight from Eltonstock to New York, or even to Australia.

Just the same, she couldn't rest until she had looked up the London directory, in case a new volume had come out with his name in it.

And there it was. In Harley Street, just as his mother had wanted.

Julie felt dizzy with excitement. He was here, in London, a stone's throw from her.

Nothing in the world would have stopped her from just going to look at the place. It was late Friday, with the week-end ahead, and more than likely he had departed already, for wherever he spent his week-ends, but Julie had to see the place where the days in between were spent.

A trim house with a newly-painted door, freshly polished brass knocker, bell-pushes, and letter-box, and among all the other names was his. Adam Hollidge.

She leaned against the railings, looking up at the windows, all shining clean, with their nice nylon nets blocking out the world inside. She yearned at it all, imprinting it on her memory for when she went away. Now all she had to do was to look up the news-paper report of the inquest tomorrow, and she need stay in London no longer.

She turned away at last, wondering with something like dismay where she would go, with so many places to choose, and no ties, no allegiances, no one with a duty to. A ship without an anchor, a dog without a lead, a child lost. Any of those things might have applied, she thought, with a catch in her throat.

Suddenly her bad leg gave way, and power-less to help herself, she fell flat on her face.

She heard running footsteps. She was try-ing to scramble to her feet, horrified at attracting attention for fear of being sent to hospital, when a man bent over her and hauled her to her feet, and she looked up into Adam's face.

'Julie?' he said thickly. 'Are you hurt? I was getting out of my car and I saw you go down. Can you walk? Here, let me help you to my consulting rooms. I was going back myself.'

The pain in her leg blotted everything else out. Somehow he managed to get her up the steps, and the door open, and then they were inside. Once the door was closed behind them he swung her light form up into his arms and carried her into the room on the left and lay her on the couch.

'Oh I didn't want to see you any more,' she moaned.

'Don't talk. Here, drink this. Now, just lie quietly while I take my coat off, then I'll have a look at that leg.'

Adam in a brisk mood was never to be denied. Whatever she had felt about going back to the hospital, he had her in an ambulance in no time at all. Despite her protests, she was admitted to his new hospital, and she didn't need to be told what was going to happen to her. He had always wanted a chance to do something to that leg, and now it had been given to him and there was very little she could do about it. She played with the idea of refusing to sign the consent form, but the thought of being liable to fall flat on her face like that, when Adam wasn't there to save her, was a frightening one. She recalled how her leg had nearly let her down when crossing the road, the first day she had gone to lunch with Neville Stannard, and she couldn't face the grim thought of it happening again.

The first time Adam had a chance to talk to her alone was the following evening. She was in a private room. The hospital was so close to the river that she could hear the noises of shipping and cranes on the wharves, all the fascinating sound of London being busy. But now she didn't mind, because for the moment she was in someone else's care, and it was so nice, however transient, to feel that she was anchored a little.

Somewhere near at hand there had been a voice untunefully repeating the latest hit of the pops. Julie had heard it through her headphones earlier on. It turned out to be a ward orderly. She bustled in with an emptied waste-paper basket and went out with a cheerful wink at Julie, never ceasing her muttering the song under her breath:

'I want you, honey
But I'm poor and lonely.
I'd bring you diamonds
But love is the only
Jewel I bring you
But I'll play my part.
I've got no diamonds.
But I bring my heart.'

Silly doggerel, but the message got through and it made Julie feel lonely again.

She put on her headphones, but a group were belting it out, with the third line postponed while the drums beat an extra two bars for effect.

She tore off the headphones and lay with her eyes closed. He could she go through with this, loving Adam as she did, when all he cared about was his place in Harley Street, and his reaching the top?

And then he came in.

She watched him unsmilingly as he pulled up a chair and took one of her hands. 'Well, Julie?' he began.

'Hello,' she said.

'Much water under the bridge, my dear,' he said, and a sad little smile touched his lips. 'Did you find all the bright promise in that new life you wanted?'

'The bright *what?*' she asked blankly.

'When my mother was ill, we talked about you. I'm afraid I got angry because I didn't want you to go to Miss Kemp's, but my mother made me see it from your point of view. Of course it was better for you to break right away. You made that clear to her on the station, and I saw it, too, when she told me. I didn't mean to try and keep you in Fleckbury— I just thought it would be a good thing for you to keep you under my wing. But my mother made me see that the Miss Kemp angle was just a convenient story to give to old Howe, who doesn't like letting his employees go. Where *did* you go, Julie, and what were you doing in Harley Street?'

She stared, speechless. Had his mother lied to him? Was she as fanatical about his future as that?

'I don't understand,' she said at last. 'I went to Miss Kemp's. Your mother arranged it all. I had nowhere else to go. I was just agreeing with her that it would be a good thing to get away from everything.'

'You *went* to Miss Kemp's?' he asked, his forehead creasing into an angry frown.

'Where else had I to go? Oh, I suppose you don't know what happened to make me run quickly from the hospital that day.' After the slightest hesitation she told Adam about Boyd's threats, and her acquiescence, because she didn't know the truth about Reuben Floy's death and she was afraid Boyd might be speaking the truth about his witness. She told him about Rosalind's part in it, and the way things had gone wrong and that she hadn't been able to switch the Mendellini Collar after all.

'I didn't have a chance to look at it, so I had no idea whether it was the copy or the original. I just wanted to get it over with and get out of there. I'm sorry, but I only heard the day before yesterday that your wife had been killed, driving Boyd's car,' and she told

Adam how she had, on impulse, telephoned Gideon, and of how he had rushed to write to her about it.

Adam couldn't believe it. 'But I thought – oh, my dear, I didn't get in touch with you, because I didn't know you were at Miss Kemp's. I thought–'

'I know your mother was ill and didn't recover,' she said gently, 'but could you bear to think back as to what she did say about me?'

Adam thought, and shook his head. 'I was angry and asked her what she could have been about, sending you to that dreadful house, that dull existence, and my mother said – to the best of my recollection – something like, "did you really think I'd send her to Miss Kemp?"'

'But she didn't actually say she wasn't sending me there, did she? She was doing her best for you.'

'Her best!' he exploded.

'She told me that she wanted more than anything else for you to have no encumbrances to your career. She wanted you to get out of Fleckbury, alone, to rise to the top. She was only doing her best for you in the only way she knew. And you can't blame her for wanting to put an end to what seemed to her an unsuitable friendship with me, now can you?'

He looked so angry. He got up and went

to stare out of the window. Julie watched his back, and though what a strong back it was, what a strong head; how wrong she had been to think that his was not a face to remember. It had been stamped, every detail of it, on her mind for so long.

He turned suddenly and caught her looking at him. He came back to her. 'My mother didn't know – it wasn't friendship I was offering you. It was more than that, and when I was free, the bottom fell out of my world, because you'd gone, heaven knew where, and all I could think of was that it was too late.'

He took her hand again. 'It is too late, isn't it, Julie? You didn't look pleased to see me. Perhaps I was wrong – perhaps you never did look really pleased to see me. Maybe I just imagined it.'

'How could you have imagined it? You don't listen to me,' she said thickly. 'Look at the way I threw myself at you that time, at the lake at Chagwell Heights, and got soundly rebuffed for my pains. Don't you remember? Well, nothing's changed, Adam. Nothing ever will. It's always been you. Only–'

He tried to draw her into his arms, but she held him off.

'No, listen, there's something I've remembered. Oh, how awful! It was a thing I meant to do – I might be responsible for someone's

250

death–' and rather incoherently she told him about Boyd's threats and of how she had intended to go and look up the newspaper account of her old friend's end, while she was pinned under the car.

'You've still been worrying about that, after all this time? Oh, my dear, if only I'd known. If I'd had any idea that that cousin of yours was doing this to you– Julie, I had it looked up. I phoned a solicitor friend, at the time you first told me about Boyd, and you were so vague about it. He looked up the account of the inquest and told me.'

'Why didn't you tell me?' Julie cried. 'What was it?'

'I didn't think I'd be doing the right thing in opening it all up again, as you never said any more about it. Reuben Floy collapsed with heart failure. No doubt from shock at seeing the car coming towards him, but my dear, you didn't touch him.'

He held her close to him until she had stopped crying. And then he kissed her.

'Julie, will you marry me?' he asked her.

She nodded, smiling through her tears.

'And you won't hold it against me if I can't manage to do something about your leg?'

'No, I won't, but it wouldn't be much good if I did, would it? You insisted on doing it! I can see you're going to be the boss of the outfit!'

'Well, that's me,' he said ruefully. 'And I

haven't a very happy past record. I didn't make Rosalind happy.'

'I can't help that,' Julie said, nestling her head against him. 'I want you– I always have since I first saw you – and I'm perfectly happy with you as you are.'

The publishers hope that this book has given you enjoyable reading. Large Print Books are especially designed to be as easy to see and hold as possible. If you wish a complete list of our books please ask at your local library or write directly to:

Dales Large Print Books
Magna House, Long Preston,
Skipton, North Yorkshire.
BD23 4ND

This Large Print Book, for people
who cannot read normal print,
is published under the auspices of

THE ULVERSCROFT FOUNDATION